Peter Foreman

Bizarre Tales

The Boy Who Couldn't Sleep

and Other Stories

Editors: Rebecca Raynes
Design: Nadia Maestri
Illustrations: Mario Benvenuto, Sara Blasigh

© 1998 Cideb Editrice, Genoa

First edition: February 1998

All rights reserved. No part of this book may be reproduced, stored in a retrieval system, or transmitted, in any form or by any means, electronic, mechanical, photocopying, recording or otherwise, without the written permission of the publisher.

We would be happy to receive your comments and suggestions, and give you any other information concerning our material.
Our e-mail and web-site addresses are:
editorial@blackcat-cideb.com
www.blackcat-cideb.com
www.cideb.it

ISBN 88-7754-771-5

Printed in Italy by Litoprint, Genoa

Contents

	Introduction	5
1.	Spirits of Place	7
	ACTIVITIES	19
2.	God's Secret	27
	ACTIVITIES	41
3.	The Boy Who Couldn't Sleep	49
	ACTIVITIES	67
4.	Fiona's Spring Dress	75
	ACTIVITIES	91
5.	A Twentieth-Century Malady	99
	ACTIVITIES	115

 These symbols indicate the beginning and end of the extracts linked to the listening activities.

Introduction

I try to write stories that say something interesting because I want you to think and talk about them. I mean that I usually write with a message. Strange things are interesting and they often make us think. This was why I decided to write tales of the bizarre; I could put a message in each story. When you have finished them, why not try to match the stories with the messages? You will find this activitiy on page 122.
Have fun!

Peter Foreman

Before reading

1 Have you ever been to America? Yes? Write a few sentences about it. No? What ideas do you have about it?

2 Read lines 1-28 and answer the questions.

a. What or who are 'them'? Give your own ideas.

b. Have you got the same things as Andy? Tick the appropriate box.
- [ ] your own TV
- [ ] your own video
- [ ] your own computer
- [ ] video games, films, electronic games etc.

c. Do you ever feel bored like Andy?

d. What is going to happen to Andy in America? Write some ideas.

Spirits of Place

It was Andy who first saw them that night but he didn't want to say anything. Then it was too late and they were already in the house. His Mum and Dad were there but they said later, 'We didn't see anything strange but we heard Uncle Paul's terrible scream!' 1 When Aunt Julie finally saw them she was very frightened and she couldn't speak. Andy's cousin Patty didn't see or hear anything; she was out at a party. And Uncle Paul? Well, he didn't believe Andy when he told him they were in the house. So he went to look with the torch and... poor Uncle Paul!

That summer Andy and his parents were staying with

---

1. **scream** : a long, loud cry of fear or terror.

BiZArrE TaleS

their American relatives ¹ on Long Island, New York. The
large, comfortable house near Amityville stood
in beautiful gardens with tall trees and
flowerbeds ² and green lawns. ³ Uncle Paul,
a doctor in a private clinic, was rich.
Andy's parents weren't rich, but Andy
had everything he wanted. At home in
Italy he had his own TV, video and computer.
His room was full of video games and films
and all kinds of electronic things. His parents
bought him anything he wanted.

But Andy was 14 now and he was often very
bored. ⁴ He had done all the computer games and seen all
the videos and there wasn't anything new. He felt that life
didn't have any surprises.

And then he came to America.

His American relatives were kind. He didn't speak English
very well so sometimes they spoke in Italian. They called
him Andy (his name was Andrea) and made him feel
welcome. Uncle Paul showed him his expensive computer
and said, 'Use it when you want to, Andy.' But Andy didn't

---

1. **relatives** : people who are connected by marriage or family.
2. **flowerbeds** : places in a garden where flowers are cultivated.
3. **lawns** [lɔːnz] : areas of cultivated grass in gardens or parks.
4. **bored** [bɔːd] : not interested in or excited by anything.

Spirits of Place

want to. He knew all about computers. They were boring now.

But then, when he went out for a walk one day, he noticed some strange things. The elegant mansions,[1] the big green lawns, and the beautiful cadillacs looked so clean and new. Even the pavements and roads were in perfect condition. And there wasn't a speck[2] of rubbish[3] anywhere.

Andy noticed all this because he was bored. He was looking for something interesting and surprising. After Italy the silent, empty streets surprised him a lot. Nobody walked around the streets.

And then he noticed something else. His American relatives never opened the windows of their house. These were always locked and there was a security alarm system.[4] What were Uncle Paul and Aunt Julie scared of? And then outside in the street it was hot, but inside the house it was

1. **mansions** : large, expensive houses, often in the country.
2. **speck** : very small particle.
3. **rubbish** [rʌbɪʃ] : useless things that people throw away.
4. **alarm system** : electrical device that makes a loud sound to warn of danger or intrusion into the house.

Bizarre Tales

cool [1] because there was air conditioning. And it was very quiet. You couldn't hear anything from outside. To Andy there was something strange about all this. He felt that the atmosphere of this clean, quiet island was frightening.

One morning Uncle Paul said, 'Would you like to see some real live [2] Indians today, Andy?'

Andy understood that his uncle wanted to show him the Indians so he said yes and tried to smile. He knew all about Indians from his comics and films. Indians didn't interest him now. Indians were for kids. But on the way to the reservation [3] Uncle Paul told him that the name of the Indian tribe was Shinnecock. Andy had never heard the name before. I've never seen a real live Shinnecock Indian, he thought. Perhaps it'll be interesting.

When they reached the reservation, Uncle Paul parked his car outside a wooden cabin. [4] This was the ticket office.

'Hey, where are all the tourists?' he said. 'It looks closed.'

---

1. **cool** : not warm; slightly cold.
2. **live** [laɪv] : (here) authentic.
3. **reservation** : area of land given to an Indian tribe for living in.
4. **wooden** [wodən] **cabin** : small structure like a house, made of wood.

Spirits of Place

He knocked on the window of the ticket office. It was opened by a young woman with the brown face and dark eyes of an Indian.

'We're closed!' she said angrily and shut the window.

Back in the car Uncle Paul said, 'Did you see that? She was really mad [1] at us. These Indians don't like us and they don't want us on their land. Sometimes they're dangerous too. A couple of weeks ago they attacked some tourists and the police came.' Uncle Paul looked around quickly. His eyes were scared. 'Come on, let's go!' he said.

So he drove to a quiet place by the sea. They had fish for lunch and then they went for a trip on a fishing boat. Andy found this boring. All the time he was thinking about the Indians. He couldn't forget that scared look in Uncle Paul's eyes. Why was he so scared of the Indians? Andy was surprised. Here was something really interesting!

On the way home he said, 'Did Long Island belong to the Indians once?'

'Belong? Well, yes and no. They lived here but that was a long time ago when all this was wild [2] country. There was

---

1. **mad** : (American English) angry.
2. **wild** : (here) uncultivated.

Bizarre Tales

nothing here – only forest – and they didn't own ¹ it legally. Now it belongs to us – the American people.'

Andy looked at Uncle Paul. 'Maybe the Indians will take it back one day.' He didn't know why he said this.

The scared look came back into Uncle Paul's eyes.

'Oh no, Andy, I don't think so. That's not possible. No, that'll never never happen. It's too late now. Hell, ² that's a crazy thing to say, Andy! Unbelievable!' ³

And Uncle Paul laughed. But Andy looked at him and saw the fear in his eyes.

That night when Andy went to bed, he got another surprise. His room had a window that overlooked ⁴ the back garden. Of course the window was locked. Next to it was the air-conditioning unit. ⁵ The room was cold and Andy couldn't sleep, so he got up and went to turn off the unit. At that moment he thought he saw somebody in the garden.

He looked hard but he couldn't see much. Then suddenly he saw something under the dark trees. At first it looked like smoke, but when it came into the moonlight, Andy couldn't believe his eyes. It was an Indian!

1. **own** [əʊn] : (here) possess.
2. **Hell** : (here) an exclamation, like Damn!
3. **Unbelievable** [ʌnbɪˈliːvəbəl] : incredible.
4. **overlooked** : had a view of.
5. **air-conditioning unit** : part of an electronic system that controls the temperature of the air in a building.

Bizarre Tales

The figure [1] went into the shadows. In a few moments another Indian came. He was walking slowly, like a hunter.
115 And again he disappeared [2] among the dark trees. Soon a third Indian came, and then another... Andy saw about twenty Indians. They had painted faces and looked horribly savage [3] and ferocious. Their eyes and teeth shone in the moonlight. They all had bows and arrows, [4] knives and tomahawks. [5] Silently they came and silently they went. Andy watched, fascinated but scared. Then some big clouds covered
125 the moon and the garden became dark. Andy looked and looked but there were no more Indians.

At first he thought he was dreaming. He wanted to go out into the garden but that was impossible. The house was locked up. So he sat on his bed
130 while the figures of the Indians moved in front of his eyes like pictures on a computer screen or in a film.

1. **figure** [fɪɡə] : form, shape.
2. **disappeared** : went away where Andy couldn't see him.
3. **savage** [sævɪdʒ] : barbarous, cruel.
4. **bows** [bəʊz] **and arrows** :
5. **tomahawks** [tɒməˌhɔːks] :

Spirits of Place

Were the figures in the garden real? Were they only in his mind? Or were they ghosts?

Suddenly a great crash of thunder [1] made him jump. There was a flash of lightning [2] and more thunder. Rain began to fall on the roof. Andy heard voices and opened the door. Uncle Paul and Aunt Julie were checking that the doors and windows were safe.

'A storm is coming,' said Aunt Julie. 'You okay, Andy?'

Uncle Paul said, 'The wind is shaking the house. [3] It's unbelievable!'

Now the rain was crashing on the roof and the windows. Then there was a bright flash of lightning and thunder that shook [4] the walls. The lights suddenly went out. The house was in darkness.

'Quick, quick! Get the torch!' Aunt Julie shouted in panic. 'It's in the garage.'

The garage was connected to the house by a door in the kitchen. Uncle Paul tried to find his way there in the dark. He bumped into [5] things and nearly fell down some steps. Aunt Julie and Andy waited. When the lightning flashed again, Andy saw her face. It was white with fear.

---

1. **crash of thunder** : loud noise in the sky during a storm.
2. **flash of lightning** : bright light during a storm produced by electricity in the clouds.
3. **shaking [ʃeɪkɪŋ] the house** : making the house vibrate.
4. **shook [ʃʊk]** : vibrated. See note 3. The past of the verb 'to shake'.
5. **bumped into** : walked against accidentally.

BiZArrE TaLeS

'You okay, Andy?' she asked every five seconds.

155　Andy was okay. He was having a great time.[1] He went to the window and looked out. And by the light of another flash of lightning he saw – hundreds of Indians! The garden was full of Indians, and they were 160　dancing a war dance in the storm.

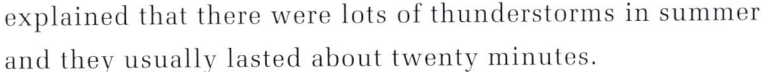

'The torch is okay.' said Uncle Paul's voice. He came into the kitchen with the torch on.

'Oh – oh, thank God!' said Aunt 165　Julie.

At that moment Andy's parents came into the kitchen. They couldn't sleep. Uncle Paul explained that there were lots of thunderstorms in summer 170　and they usually lasted about twenty minutes.

'But it's the first time the lights have gone,' said Aunt Julie in a scared voice.

'Don't be scared,' said Uncle Paul. 'Everybody sit down and we'll have cup of...'

175　He was going to say coffee, but of course there was no electricity. Nothing was working: the cooker, the fridge, the

---

1. **He was having a great time** : he was enjoying himself.

Spirits of Place

phone, the TV and video, the computer, the air-conditioning, the security alarm – all, all dead!

When the storm passed, there was silence. Deep silence. Everybody sat at the table and Uncle Paul began to tell bad jokes. Nobody laughed. Aunt Julie was very scared.

'The lights will come on soon, won't they? she asked every five seconds.

One hour... and a half... The lights didn't come on. Aunt Julie was nearly hysterical. Andy's parents were becoming nervous. Uncle Paul stopped telling bad jokes. Andy asked himself many times, 'Shall I tell them?' And each time he thought, 'No. They won't believe me.' He looked at the frightened faces around him and decided to say nothing. He went to the window for the tenth time to look for the Indians. Black, black night. The garden was invisible.

'Oh my God!' Aunt Julie suddenly screamed. 'The torch, the torch! It's going out!'

She was right. The torchlight was weaker. The next moment Andy saw something in the hall outside the kitchen. A dark shape was moving around like a shadow.

'Uncle Paul,' he said quietly. 'I think there are Indians in the house.'

BiZArrE TaLeS

'Indians? What are you talking about, Andy? You're seeing things.¹ You're scared...'

Just then Aunt Julie screamed and pointed² into the hall.

'What is it?' Uncle Paul said, very frightened.

But Aunt Julie couldn't speak; she was frozen³ with fear.

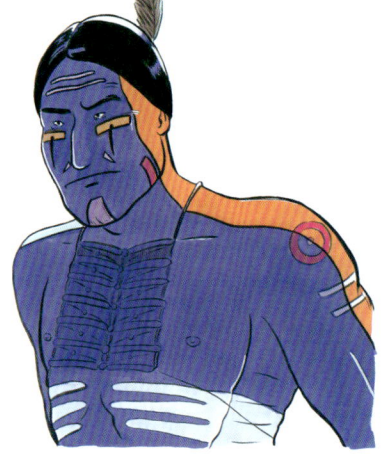

'Wait here everybody. I'm going to take a look around,' said Uncle Paul. And he went out with the torch.

Now the kitchen was dark.

'Oh, don't!... Don't go!' cried poor Aunt Julie. Her body was shaking with terror.

There was a moment of silence; and then came a long, horrible scream of agony that filled the whole house.⁴

---

1. **'You're seeing things'** : 'You're imagining things.'
2. **pointed** : indicated with her finger.
3. **frozen** [frəʊzən] : (here) rigid.
4. **the whole** [həʊl] **house** : every room in the house.

ACTIVITIES

After reading

1 Put the sentences in the correct order to make a summary of the story. Write 1,2,3 etc. in the box. (Some are done for you.)

- a. ☐ So one day he went for a walk.
- b. ☐ Andy and his parents were staying with American relatives.
- c. **7** Then one day Uncle Paul took him to an Indian reservation.
- d. ☐ Then a storm came and the lights went out.
- e. ☐ He noticed that the streets were clean and empty.
- f. ☐ That night Andy saw some Indians in the garden.
- g. ☐ The storm passed but the lights didn't come on.
- h. ☐ After a few days Andy became bored.
- i. **10** He thought that perhaps he was dreaming or seeing ghosts.
- j. **4** He was looking for something interesting.
- k. ☐ An hour and a half later he saw an Indian in the house and told Uncle Paul.
- l. ☐ And he felt that there was something strange and frightening about the atmosphere of Long Island.
- m. ☐ Andy was surprised because his uncle seemed scared of the Indians.
- n. ☐ Uncle Paul went to investigate and there was a terrible scream.
- o. **12** When Andy looked out of the window again, he saw hundreds of Indians dancing in the garden.

Now rewrite the sentences in their correct order in your exercise book to make a paragraph.

ACTIVITIES

2 Read lines 103-26 and put the pictures in the order that they are mentioned. Write 1,2,3 etc. in the correct box.

a.
b.
c.
d.
e.
f.

ACTIVITIES

3 A. Who in the story...

   a. didn't want to say anything about the Indians?
   ....
   b. bought Andy anything he wanted?
   ....
   c. sometimes spoke to Andy in Italian?
   ....
   d. said angrily, 'We're closed!'?
   ....
   e. said, 'You okay, Andy?' every five seconds?
   ....
   f. danced in the storm?
   ....
   g. screamed a long, horrible scream of agony?
   ....

B. If possible, write why they did or said these things.

   a. ....
   b. ....
   c. ....
   d. ....
   e. ....
   f. ....
   g. ....

Check your answers in the text.

ACTIVITIES

4 Complete the sentences with an appropriate adjective from the box. Be careful – there are too many adjectives!

> expensive   dark   large   silent   bored   savage   nervous
> clean   empty   strange   ferocious   comfortable
> electronic   interesting   new   scared   frightening   rich

a. Andy often felt ………………… . In fact, he was looking for something ………………… .
b. Uncle Paul was …………………, but Andy's parents weren't.
c. Uncle Paul had a …………………, ………………… house.
d. Uncle Paul's computer was ………………… .
e. The mansions, the lawns, and the cadillacs looked ………………… and ………………… .
f. Andy was surprised because the streets were ………………… and ………………… .
g. Why was Uncle Paul so ………………… of the Indians?
h. Andy thought that the atmosphere of Long Island was ………………… and ………………… .
i. The Indians in the garden looked ………………… and ………………… .

5 Complete the sentences with the words in the box.

> anywhere   anything   somebody   nothing
> anybody   something   nobody

a. At first Andy didn't want to tell ………………… about the Indians.
b. He wanted to find ………………… interesting because he was bored.

ACTIVITIES

c. On Long Island Andy was surprised because .... walked around the streets.

d. And there wasn't a speck of rubbish ....

e. Inside the house it was quiet; you couldn't hear .... from outside.

f. There was no electricity so .... was working: the cooker, the fridge, etc.

g. When Andy saw an Indian in the hall, he said, 'There's .... in the house, Uncle Paul, and I think it's an Indian.'

6 Complete the sentences with the correct preposition.

> outside   in front of   in (x 2)   on (x 2)
> at (x 2)   inside   next to   under

a. Uncle Paul's house was .... Long Island.

b. Uncle Paul worked .... a private clinic.

c. That evening Patty was .... a party.

d. Andy's window was .... the air-conditioning unit.

e. .... in the streets it was hot, but .... the house it was cool.

f. There was a figure .... the garden .... the dark trees.

g. Andy sat .... his bed and saw the Indians .... his eyes like pictures.

h. Everybody was sitting .... the table and Uncle Paul was telling jokes.

ACTIVITIES

7 A. Find the 13 members of a family in the word puzzle and write them in the correct column in the table. Two have been done for you.

B	E	A	F	O	J	S	V	S	X
R	K	M	J	C	Z	I	G	O	R
O	W	Q	C	O	U	S	I	N	Y
T	Y	H	Z	U	N	T	P	I	D
H	G	U	O	S	C	E	Y	E	V
E	T	S	K	I	L	R	D	C	G
R	J	B	J	N	E	P	H	E	W
C	D	A	U	G	H	T	E	R	I
A	U	N	T	W	N	F	Q	Z	F
U	B	D	M	O	T	H	E	R	E

Male	Female
cousin	
	sister

One word is missing, isn't it? Can you guess what it is? Write it in the correct place in the table.

B. Now write sentences with some of the words in 7A, like the example.

a. Aunt Julie / Andy — Aunt Julie is Andy's aunt.
b. Andy / Uncle Paul — ....
c. Patty / Andy — ....
d. Uncle Paul / Aunt Julie — ....
e. Aunt Julie / Patty — ....

ACTIVITIES

8 Answer one of these questions.

   a. You are Andy. Write a letter to your friend in Italy and describe what happened after the long, horrible scream.
   b. You are Patty and you came home about an hour later. Next day a journalist interviewed you on TV. Write the dialogue between you and the journalist. Begin like this:

   Journalist: Where were you when this happened last night, Patty?

   Patty: ....

9 In your opinion, does the story say anything about America? Can you write a few ideas?

A C T I V I T I E S

Before reading

1 Which of these words do you associate with heaven and hell? Write them in the table.

light   underground   bad   angel   God   fire
smoke   unhappy   black   the devil   blue
garden   dark   happy   sky   good   red

HEAVEN	HELL

2 In your opinion, would these people be in heaven or hell? Can you say why?

Al Capone ....
Walt Disney ....
Adolf Hitler ....
Robin Hood ....
John Lennon ....
Marilyn Monroe ....
Dracula ....
Snow White ....
Mahatma Gandhi ....

God's Secret

It looked like a beautiful palace or a very big hotel. But it wasn't made of stone; it was made of clouds: immense, milky-white ¹ clouds. When I reached ² the doors, they opened automatically; but perhaps they floated ³ open – I can't say.

I entered an enormous hall. It was so high and so wide that I felt dizzy. ⁴ It seemed that I was standing on air. A bright light – like sunlight but not sunlight – reflected from the walls of cloud – or were they made of snow? Then, far

---

1. **milky-white** : (compound adjective) white like milk.
2. **reached** : arrived at.
3. **floated** [fləʊtɪd] : (here) moved freely in the air.
4. **dizzy** [dɪzi] : a sensation like vertigo when the head seems to go round and round.

BiZArrE TAleS

10 away on the other side of the hall, I saw somebody behind a large reception desk. [1]

'This is like a hotel,' I thought as I walked towards [2] it. 'But what a hotel! It's beautiful! This *must* be heaven.'

It was a long walk but I was smiling to
15 myself all the way. I felt very happy now. I thought, you tried to be a good person all your life. You always did your best to help people, to do good things, and to love your neighbour. [3] You always *knew* that you
20 would go to heaven. And now here you are!

Yes, I felt so happy that I wanted to sing. I think I *did* sing! Quietly, of course. I didn't want to disturb the peace and silence of heaven.

25 I stopped at the reception desk where a man of about forty-five was waiting for me. He wore a green suit of shiny [4] material, like plastic, and a beautiful golden cloak. [5] He looked up at me.

---

1. **reception desk** : place where clients are received when they arrive.
2. **towards** [tə'wɔːdz] : in the direction of.
3. **love your neighbour** [neɪbə] : be kind and friendly to people you meet. Usually, your neighbour lives in the house next to you.
4. **shiny** [ʃaɪnɪ] : reflecting light. An adjective from the verb 'to shine'.
5. **golden cloak** [kləʊk] : a long piece of material without sleeves, worn round the shoulders. Here, of a yellow colour like gold.

God's Secret

'Name?'

I told him. He found it on a computer.

'We need some details [1] about you,' he said. 'When were you born?'

I told him.

'When did you die? The exact time, please.'

'Early this morning, I think. About 5.30. But I'm not sure about it because I was dead.' I smiled.

The receptionist looked at me coldly. He was English. Calm, polite.

'Occupation?'

I told him. Then he wanted details about my family and friends, my habits, my favourite food – in fact, everything about my life. It was like an interrogation. But I felt very relaxed and friendly. [2] I wanted to have a chat. [3]

'Wonderful place you've got here!' I began. 'It's exactly as I imagined it.'

---

1. **details** ['diːteɪlz] : small facts.
2. **friendly** [frendlɪ] : amicable, like a friend.
3. **chat** : informal conversation.

Bizarre Tales

The man didn't even look at me. 'Imagined *what*, may I ask?'

'Heaven of course! I'm very happy to be here. There's only one bad thing: all my best friends will be in hell.' And I laughed at this bad joke.

'This is *not* heaven, sir,' the man said, very polite but cold. 'This is only reception.'

I was shocked. 'But it *must* be heaven!'

'*Why* must it?'

'Because... because... well, you've heard the details of my life. I mean, I've always been a good man and if you're good, you'll go to heaven, but if you're...'

'Everybody says that, sir,' the man interrupted. 'I know you all think that on earth, but we have a different logic here – for practical reasons. Think of the problems if good people always go to heaven and bad people always go to hell. There will be very few people in heaven and too many people in hell. There isn't enough room [1] in hell. So we have a more practical system. Everybody must take his or her chance.'

'Chance? What do you mean?' I was beginning to feel a bit frightened.

At that moment the computer buzzed [2] and a piece of paper came out.

---

1. **room** : (here) space.
2. **buzzed** [bʌzd] : made a low vibrating sound (like a bee!).

God's Secret

'Here's your reception form, sir. And this is your green card. Go through¹ the doors behind me and walk along the road. You will see two large gates. In front of them are some slot² machines. Insert your green card into the left-hand³ slot and you will see two dice⁴ in the display window. Pull the handle⁵ and when the dice stop, the machine will deliver a white card for any number from one to six and a black card for any number from seven to twelve. The white card opens the gate on the right, the black card opens the left. The left goes to hell, the right to heaven.'

I couldn't believe my ears and I just stared⁶ at him. Then I became angry.

'But that's not fair!'⁷ I shouted.

---

1. **through** [θruː] : (prep.) from one side to the other.
2. **slot** : a narrow aperture. Usually, slot machines are operated by money put into a slot.
3. **left-hand** : on the left.
4. **dice** [daɪs] :
5. **handle** :
6. **stared** : looked with his eyes wide open.
7. **'But that's not fair!'** : 'That doesn't follow the rules!'

Bizarre Tales

'It's as fair as we can make it, sir.'

'But it's just chance! Luck! Accident! It's a lottery!'

'Yes, sir. But it's God's orders and we can't change it.'

'God's orders!' I shouted, furious. 'But it means that Jack the Ripper [1], for example, could be in heaven!'

'Jack the Ripper? I've heard the name before. Let me see.' The receptionist opened a large file. [2]

'Yes, Jack the Ripper. He arrived about a hundred earth years ago. I don't remember very well but I think he was quite [3] pleased with our system.'

'I'm sure he was!' I said angrily. 'And I'm sure he went to heaven!' Then I looked quickly at the clerk. 'Well? Did he?'

'I can't tell you that, sir. You see, we don't know. Nobody knows. It's God's secret.'

'God's secret?' I cried, 'Oh God, no, no! I'm not going to spend eternity with Jack the Ripper. It's not fair!' And I stamped my foot [4] on the floor like an angry child.

1. **Jack the Ripper** : the name of a man who killed five women in Whitechapel, London, in 1888. His identify is unknown.
2. **file** [faɪl] : a kind of book or cover for keeping papers in order.
3. **quite** [kwaɪt] : (here) sufficiently.
4. **stamped my foot** : brought my foot down hard.

God's Secret

'You must take your chance like everybody else, sir,' the man said coldly.

'But don't you understand? All my life I tried to be a good man!'

The man looked embarrassed. 'I'm sorry but that is not relevant to the laws [1] of the universe.'

'What laws? What do you mean?'

'If I remember well, there was a Mr Albert Einstein who arrived about forty years ago. He was a good man too, I believe and, like you, he was very upset [2] by our system. He couldn't accept it. He said that he didn't believe that God plays dice. I told him that God certainly plays dice and that it was the fundamental reality of the universe. Yes, Mr Einstein was very unhappy about that because he had helped to discover it – so he said.'

I didn't answer; I was too upset to speak. I took the form and the green card and walked quickly to the doors behind the reception desk. They floated open.

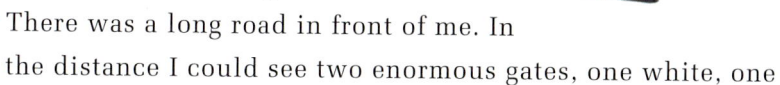

There was a long road in front of me. In the distance I could see two enormous gates, one white, one

---

1. **laws** [lɔːz] : (here) facts describing what always happens (in the universe).
2. **upset** [ʌpˈset] : disturbed or distressed in his mind.

Bizarre Tales

135 black. They were made of beautiful heavy crystal glass that shone¹ like jewellery. ²

I walked along the road. It was very silent. On each side of me were great clouds that trembled and changed in a soft wind. Even the light seemed to change from brightness to
140 shadow and back again.

I came to the gates. When I looked at the black gate on the left, my heart stopped. What was behind it? *Who* was behind it? Then I looked at the gate on my right and trembled. Who or what was behind heaven's gate? I inserted my green card
145 in one of the slot machines. There was a buzzing sound and the display window showed two dice. My hand went up to pull the handle.

'Not yet, not yet!' I said to myself. 'I want to think. I want to sit down and wait a bit. I want to take my time.' So I sat
150 on the road and began to talk to myself. 'Oh, this is terrible! I never smoked, I never drank, I never gambled, ³ I never stole any money, I never hurt ⁴ anybody... Of course I was careful about my health ⁵ and I looked after my money ⁶ like everybody else. I wasn't stupid! But now... ! I could be with

---

1. **shone** [ʃɒn] : reflected light. The Past of the verb 'to shine'.
2. **jewellery** [dʒuːəlri] : for example, rings, necklaces, etc.
3. **gambled** : played cards or other games for money.
4. **hurt** [hɜːt] : caused pain or injury (to someone).
5. **my health** [helθ] : my physical condition.
6. **looked after my money** : didn't spend too much money.

Bizarre Tales

thieves, murderers – politicians! – for the rest of eternity. It's really terrible!'

And so I sat there and talked like a lunatic. Sometimes I looked at the handle of the slot machine which was waiting for me, and I trembled.

'Well, it's better to be in heaven even if Jack the Ripper is there. People say that heaven is a beautiful place. Oh, God, dear God, *please* let me get a white card!'

So I prayed [1] for a white card and after a while I felt much better, more optimistic. I felt that God was on my side. [2] I stood up, walked to the machine and pulled the handle down quickly. The dice began to spin. [3] I closed my eyes; opened them. The first dice stopped at number two. My heart beat fast with hope. Then the second dice came. Five. Silence. Then like a photo from a polaroid camera the card came out. It was black. I fainted.

When I opened my eyes again, I sat still for a long time. Hot tears filled my eyes. I was going to hell!

'I knew it, I knew it!' I cried. 'I've always been unlucky!'

But what could I do? I had to enter the door on the left; I had to go to hell. I inserted my black card into a slot by the

---

1. **prayed** [preɪd] : asked God.
2. **God was on my side** : God was with me.
3. **spin** : turn quickly round and round.

God's Secret

gate. As it began to open a strange, aromatic odour came out. I went into another great hall with a reception desk at the far end. It was a long walk. The walls were made of black smoke and red flames. Behind the desk sat a pretty young blonde woman. She gave me a sweet smile.

'Hallo. May I have your reception form, please?' she said in a friendly way.

I gave her the form and she typed the information into a computer.

'Why do you look so depressed?' she asked with her sweet smile. 'You're a lucky man.'

I laughed bitterly. [1] 'Lucky?'

'Here's your room key,' she continued. 'We hope you'll like Room 206. You'll find everything in order – drinks, magazines, a change of clothes, a bottle of wine, and everything necessary for your comfort. There is a reading lounge, [2] a swimming pool, tennis courts, and a card table. [3] We hope that you will enjoy your eternity.'

I was watching her to see if she was joking behind that sweet smile.

---

1. **bitterly** : angrily and at the same time sadly.
2. **reading lounge** [laʊndʒ] : large, quiet room where people can read.
3. **card table** : a table where people play cards.

Bizarre Tales

'This *is* hell, is it?' I asked in a sarcastic voice.

'That's the official name, yes. But *we* call it Paradise Regained.¹ I suppose² you thought it would be a terrible place, but things have changed a lot. We've made it better. You'll see.'

'Who are we?'

'Oh, there are so many good, kind people here. I can't remember all their names. Let me think. Well, there's an Indian gentleman, Mr Gandhi, and a nurse called Florence Nightingale...'

'You mean those people are all here – in hell?'

'But it's not hell any more. It's the dice, you see.'

'The dice? No, I don't see.³ Please explain.'

'Well, for a long time a lot of good people scored more than six and got a black card, so now there are more good people than bad people. This doesn't happen often, of course; it's a very unusual thing and it will certainly change again. Then we'll get the usual average⁴ of about fifty good, fifty bad.'

---

1. **Paradise Regained** [pærədaɪs rɪˈɡeɪnd] : Paradise found again.
2. **I suppose** [səpəʊz] : I imagine.
3. **I don't see** : I don't understand.
4. **the usual average** : the usual number.

God's Secret

Smiling, I said, 'Has God fixed the dice – for a joke or something?'

She looked a bit shocked. 'Oh no! I'm sure God is an honest gambler.[1] It happened by accident.'

'Hm. Well, let's say it's another one of God's secrets – eh?' And I gave her a big wink.[2] 'What about Jack the Ripper? Is he here?'

'Jack the Ripper...' She looked through her file. 'No, he isn't here. He must be on the other side – in heaven.'

I laughed and laughed. 'And are they having a bad time there?'

The receptionist said quietly, 'Between you and me, we've heard that they are having a lot of trouble in heaven.'

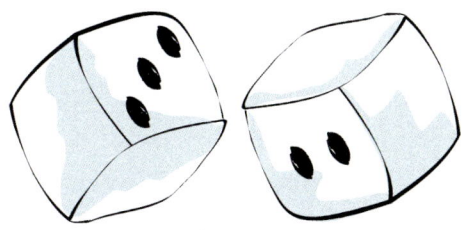

I laughed again and tears of happiness came into my eyes.

'Welcome to Paradise Regained,' said the woman with a big sweet smile. 'Have a nice eternity!'

'Thank you. This place looks better than earth...'

At that moment an intercom buzzed and the woman answered.

'Reception Three speaking. Can I help you?' As she listened

---

1. **gambler** : person who plays cards or other games for money, often as a profession.
2. **wink** : act of closing and opening one eye quickly as a signal to somebody.

Bizarre Tales

her expression changed. It became dark and anxious. 'Oh, I see. Thank you, Reception One.' She was silent.

'Anything wrong?' I asked.

'Well, as you know, the situation on earth is very turbulent at the moment and a lot of new people have arrived. Reception One says a big crowd [1] is already at the dice machine.'

'Who are they?' I had a bad feeling in my stomach.

'Reception One says it's a group of terrorists, child killers, Mafiosi, football hooligans, drug barons...'

'Stop – please stop!' I shouted.

'We can only hope that our luck continues,' she said. Her sweet smile had gone; she was looking at the entrance with frightened eyes.

I cried, 'Please God, let them all go to heaven! I pray, I pray... !'

'I'm sorry but praying won't help. It all depends on the dice.'

'And that's God's secret!' I said, laughing and crying at the same time.

While we waited, the silence was long and terrible.

---

1. **crowd** : large number of people together in one place.

ACTIVITIES

After reading

1 Listen to lines 133-70 and tick the correct picture.

ACTIVITIES

2 Match the two parts of the sentences to make a summary of the story.

a. The narrator saw
b. Inside the palace there was
c. He was happy because
d. The receptionist asked him
e. Then the receptionist told him
f. And he explained the system
g. The narrator was angry about the system because
h. At the slot machines he got a black card
i. But at the reception he wasn't sure
j. The blonde receptionist told him that there were
k. And the narrator thought that
l. He laughed and he was happy because
m. But then a lot of violent people
n. So the narrator was very agitated

1. that he wasn't in heaven.
2. a lot of good people in hell at the moment.
3. he wasn't sure now if he was going to heaven or hell.
4. he thought he was in heaven.
5. hell seemed better than heaven.
6. a beautiful palace made of clouds.
7. if he was in heaven or hell.
8. of the slot machines.
9. a lot of questions about his life.
10. and prayed that they would all go to heaven.
11. a big hall with a reception desk.
12. arrived at the gates.
13. and went to hell.
14. God had fixed the dice for a joke.

a ☐ b ☐ c ☐ d ☐ e ☐ f ☐ g ☐
h ☐ i ☐ j ☐ k ☐ l ☐ m ☐ n ☐

Now rewrite the sentences in your exercise book to make a paragraph.

ACTIVITIES

3 A. Complete the computer information about the narrator with the words in the cloud.

DECEASED N° 683
Name _____
Address _____
Age _____
Date of birth _____
Time of death _____
Occupation _____
Status _____
Family _____
Character _____

19th October 1930   married   Julian Biggs   5.30 am   three children   teacher (retired)   13a Parkside Gardens Bournemouth   67   good

B. Now write a report about the narrator using the information in 3A. Remember he's dead – use the Past Simple tense! Begin like this.

The deceased's name was ....
....
....
....
....
....
....

ACTIVITIES

4 Complete the sentences about the narrator's feelings and reactions. Check your answers in the text.

    a. He felt .... when he entered the hall because ....
....

    b. As he walked towards the reception desk he felt ....
because ....

    c. While the receptionist was asking him questions, he felt ....
.... and wanted to ....

    d. But he was .... when the receptionist told him that he wasn't in heaven.

    e. Then the receptionist told him about the slot machines and he became ....

    f. But at the slot machines he prayed and felt ....

    g. The receptionist in hell thought that he looked ....

    h. When she told him that Jack the Ripper was in heaven, he .... and felt very ....

    i. But then she said there was a big crowd at the gates and the narrator prayed because he was ....
....

5 Complete the answers with the correct possessive adjective, like the example.

a.	The narrator has got a black card.	His card is black
b.	The terrorists have got white cards.	Their
c.	The woman receptionist has got blonde hair.	
d.	We have got a better system.	
e.	I have got a new computer.	

ACTIVITIES

f. The English receptionist has got a green suit. ....
....

g. You have got a sweet smile. ....

6 First complete the sentences with the correct word. Then change the sentences using *must be* or *could be*, like the example.

a. This isn't hell. I'm sure this is <u>heaven</u>.
<u>This must be heaven.</u>

b. I'm not in <u>hell</u>. Perhaps I'm in heaven.
<u>I could be in heaven.</u>

c. The first receptionist isn't Italian. Perhaps he's ....
....

d. Julian Biggs isn't .... I'm sure he's dead.
....

e. The card isn't black. I'm sure it's ....
....

f. The blonde receptionist isn't .... I'm sure she's young.
....
....

g. The walls aren't made of stone. Perhaps they are made of ....
....

ACTIVITIES

7 This report on Julian Biggs was written when he was alive by his employer. Use it to complete the dialogue below with the correct verbs. Remember – use the Past Simple!

> **PERSONAL REPORT**
>
> Name of Employee: <u>Julian Biggs</u>
>
> Mr Biggs is a very good man. He always does his best to help other people. He has a lot of money but he often gives it away. He doesn't gamble or smoke, and he doesn't drink too much or eat too much bad food. He hasn't got any bad habits. He is polite and friendly. We understand that he is a good husband and father. He has never gone with another woman or hit his children. He is a perfect man. But there is one thing wrong about him. He knows that he is perfect and he thinks that he will go to heaven when he dies.

Receptionist: We need some more details about you, Mr Biggs. What sort of man were you?

Mr Biggs: Well, I always ¹............................. my best to help others.

Receptionist: So you ²............................. a good man?

Mr Biggs: Yes, I was. I ³............................. gamble or smoke...

Receptionist: What about drink – and food?

Mr Biggs: I never ⁴............................. too much and I never ⁵............................. bad food.

Receptionist: Are you saying that you ⁶............................. have any bad habits?

Mr Biggs: Yes, that's right.

Receptionist: Hm. And what about money? ⁷............................. you rich?

ACTIVITIES

Mr Biggs: No. I ⁸............................ quite a lot of money but I often ⁹............................ it away.

Receptionist: What a good man you were! And is it possible that you ¹⁰............................ never violent or angry?

Mr Biggs: Right! I ¹¹............................ never violent or angry. In fact, I ¹²............................ always polite and friendly.

Receptionist: Really? And were you a good husband and father too?

Mr Biggs: Yes, I ¹³............................ . I never ¹⁴............................ with another woman and I ¹⁵............................ hit my children. My wife always said that I was perfect.

Receptionist: Don't you think you were just a bit *too* perfect, Mr Biggs?

Mr Biggs: Yes, perhaps I was. When I was alive, I ¹⁶............................ that I was perfect and I ¹⁷............................ that I would certainly go to heaven. And here I am! I was right!

Receptionist: This is *not* heaven, Mr Biggs. This is only reception.

8 Answer these questions.

a. At the end of the story we don't know what is going to happen.

Do any of the new arrivals go to hell? Who? What happens after that?

Can you write your own ending? You are the narrator Julian Biggs.

b. What were your reactions to the story?

Write a letter to the author and say what you like and what you don't like about it.

Before reading

1 Answer the mini-questionnaire about sleep.

	Yes	No	Sometimes
a. Do you go to bed late?	☐	☐	☐
b. Do you get up early?	☐	☐	☐
c. Do you like going to bed?	☐	☐	☐
d. Do you like getting up?	☐	☐	☐
e. Do you usually sleep well?	☐	☐	☐
f. Do you ever suffer from insomnia?	☐	☐	☐
g. Do you ever take medicine to help you to sleep?	☐	☐	☐
h. Do you ever sleep during the day?	☐	☐	☐
i. Do you think that you need more sleep?	☐	☐	☐
j. Do you remember your dreams?	☐	☐	☐

2 Read the title and lines 1-11. Then answer the questions.

a. Can you guess why Max didn't sleep?
b. Can you say how his mother felt about this?
c. What do you think will happen to Max?

The Boy Who Couldn't Sleep

On the day that he was born Max slept [1] for most of the time. And in the first weeks of his life he slept like other babies. But when he began to look around him, he didn't sleep so much. He slept for a few hours at night and a little in the daytime. Then he stopped sleeping during the day. He was awake for twenty hours. His eyes were always open!

His mother, Samantha Price, was very surprised. She said that the world was a very interesting place and perhaps Max

---

1. **slept** : past of the verb 'to sleep'.

Bizarre Tales

wanted to see everything. She thought this was because he was intelligent.

The doctors and paediatricians were also very surprised; but they said that they didn't know why Max slept so little. Then a child psychologist studied Max's case. He said that it wasn't a very strange case. His studies showed that a lot of modern babies were sleeping less. [1] He wasn't sure why, but he had some ideas about it.

'Two hundred years ago people went to bed earlier than today,' he told Samantha. 'Generally, life was slower in the past and people slept longer. They worked a lot and they didn't have much money, so they often stayed at home after work and went to bed when it got [2] dark. You see, there was no television and there weren't any electric lights. Electric light is different from candlelight; it is brighter and it keeps you awake. [3] Babies are influenced in mysterious ways by the world. And if the world is fast, noisy, and bright, and if people often go to bed very late,

---

1. **less** : opposite of more.
2. **got** : (here) became.
3. **it keeps you awake** : it impedes sleep.

The Boy Who Couldn't Sleep

babies will feel this and they won't sleep so much.'

'Are you sure, Doctor?' Samantha said. 'I think that Max doesn't sleep because he finds the world so interesting. He's very intelligent.'

'Yes, that's possible, Mrs Price. But it's true that our society is becoming more nocturnal.' [1]

The psychologist's words surprised Samantha. She couldn't believe him. But when she told her husband Derek, he said,

'Yes, it seems crazy but our world *is* crazy! The psychologist may be right. But we'll see. Perhaps it will pass and Max will sleep like other babies.'

When Max was five, the doctors said he was a hyper-active [2] child. Every night Samantha tried to put him to bed at eight-thirty but he wasn't sleepy. [3] Samantha became angry; Derek was angry too. They shouted at Max and finally he went to bed at about half past nine. But he cried and cried, and he never fell asleep [4] before eleven o'clock. Then he woke up between four and five in the

---

1. **nocturnal** [nɒk'tɜːnəl] : active at night.
2. **hyper-active** : too active.
3. **sleepy** : ready to sleep.
4. **fell asleep** : passed into the state of sleep. 'Fell' is the Past of 'to fall'.

BiZArrE TaleS

morning and he wanted to play. Samantha and Derek were always tired and nervous.

⁵⁵ When Max was eight, he slept about two hours at night. Now Samantha and Derek went to bed while he continued to play quietly with his toys [1] or his computer. He did lots of things to pass the time and he didn't often feel bored. He ⁶⁰ liked the electronic light of the TV or computer. He was always in the light. If he was in the dark for a while, he became nervous and ⁶⁵ depressed. It seemed that he needed light.

'I think he's a mutant,' [2] Derek said one day, and he laughed. But he was half serious.

'What do you mean?' asked Samantha.

'Nature is trying to produce a new kind of human and ⁷⁰ Max is an experiment,' Derek replied, laughing. 'He's a child of the future.'

When Max was a teenager, he was awake for most of the day. At night he went to discos or all-night parties. He

1. **toys** :

2. **mutant** : a living thing that is genetically different from its parents.

The Boy Who Couldn't Sleep

watched videos or late-night films on TV, and he listened to music. He went to school every day, but he didn't get up in the morning like other children. At school his friends were surprised because he wasn't sleepy. And he worked hard. He liked learning new things and he read a lot of books. He wanted to know all about life and the world. When his friends asked him about this, he said, 'I want to understand everything. The world is a big, interesting place and life is short. We sleep too much. Sleep is a waste of time.' [1]

    Samantha and Derek were feeling better now because they usually slept well. Derek accepted Max's condition more than Samantha. He said it was true that Max was different but in other ways he was normal. He liked sport, clothes, music and girls.

    'How can you say he's normal?' said Samantha. 'A normal person can't always live in the light of day or electricity. Normal people can't live without sleep. It's impossible! Max *must* sleep or one day he will die!'

---

1. **a waste of time** : time that is not used well.

Bizarre Tales

One evening Samantha put some strong sleeping tablets [1] in Max's tea to see what would happen. When he began to look sleepy, she called Derek.

'Look!' she said excitedly. [2] 'He's going to fall asleep!'

Derek was surprised and happy. 'That's wonderful! Perhaps he's normal after all!'

'Ssh! You'll wake him up!'

After about half an hour Max opened his eyes.

'What's happening?' he said, looking around.

'You fell asleep,' said Derek with a big smile.

'Asleep? Me?' Max looked angry. 'How long?'

'About thirty minutes.'

'Oh no! I don't want to sleep. There's too much to do and see in the world. But how did I fall asleep?'

Samantha said quietly, 'I gave you some sleeping tablets.'

'You – what?' Derek shouted.

'Give them to me, Mum,' said Max.

Samantha looked very unhappy. 'Oh, you must sleep, Max! Why don't you sleep?'

---

1. **sleeping tablets** : medicine that helps you to sleep.
2. **excitedly** [ɪkˈsaɪtɪdli] : with strong emotion, usually of pleasure.

The Boy Who Couldn't Sleep

'I don't need it. When you sleep, you don't know anything. You can die in your sleep and you won't know about it. When you sleep, you can't see or hear anything. I don't like that.'

'But everybody in the world sleeps, Max!'

'I know – but not me. I want to see, hear, and know. Now give the tablets to me, Mum.'

Slowly Samantha put the packet in his hand.

But she couldn't stop herself. She was always thinking about Max's condition. One day she wrote to a famous neurologist who was an expert on sleep. Dr Somaz answered her letter, asking if he could do some tests on Max. Max said yes. After the tests, Dr Somaz said that Max's brain waves [1] were different.

'His brain produces very strong alpha waves,' the doctor explained. 'These are the normal waves when we are awake. But his brain doesn't produce any slow waves, which are normal when we are asleep. It's strange. I've never seen this before.'

'So he really doesn't need sleep?' asked Derek.

'Sometimes perhaps – just a little.'

'And he is a normal, healthy [2] person?' Samantha asked.

---

1. **brain waves** : electrical impulses produced by the organ in the head.
2. **healthy** [helθi] : well, not ill.

Bizarre Tales

'Yes, he is. But there is a problem. Sleep restores the body. If the brain is always awake, the body is not renewed. [1] And so... it will get old faster than normal...'

Samantha was looking at the doctor with big, frightened eyes. 'Do you mean that Max will die young?'

'I don't know, Mrs Price, but it's possible. I would like to do some more tests.'

Dr Somaz's tests showed that Max's body was getting old faster than normal. He was eighteen but he had the body of a man of thirty-five. Samantha and Derek were shocked.

'How long will he live?' Derek asked.

'That's a very difficult question and I don't know the answer.'

'Oh, isn't there anything we can do, Doctor?' Samantha cried. 'How can we help him?'

Dr Somaz was silent for a moment. 'Well, I know of a drug that can make him sleep. But it's a very strong drug. If he takes it for a long time – or if he takes an overdose [2] – it will kill him. And it is addictive. [3] With time he will want more of it.'

Samantha and Derek said nothing. They only looked at each other sadly.

1. **renewed** : made new.
2. **overdose** [ˈəʊvədəʊs] : too much of a medicine or drug.
3. **addictive** : it causes the person to use it as a habit.

The Boy Who Couldn't Sleep

'So if he takes this drug, he will live longer – am I right?' said Derek.

'I'm not sure, Mr Price. You see, he will be a drug addict and the drug will kill him in the end.'

'Oh God, this is terrible!' cried Samantha with big tears in her eyes. 'Which will kill him first – no sleep or the drug?'

'Again I can't be certain,' replied Dr Somaz. 'I can only say that if my calculations are right, it seems probable that without sleep he will die younger than if he takes the drug.'

After a silence, Derek said, 'We must tell poor Max all this and he can decide what he wants to do.'

'He won't take the drug,' said Samantha, shaking her head.

'Are you sure?' asked Dr Somaz.

'Yes. He says he wants to stay awake, he wants to live with his eyes open. He told us that life is too short to sleep because there is so much to learn and do. He will never take any drugs.'

'But you and Mr Price must tell him that it's better to take the drug,' Dr Somaz said. 'When he understands the problem, perhaps he will decide to take it.'

Bizarre Tales

That night Samantha and Derek talked to Max. They told him the situation and said that Dr Somaz thought it would be better for him to take the drug.

'And what do *you* think?' Max asked them.

'We agree with the doctor,' said Derek.

'No,' said Max. 'I won't take any drugs.'

'Take your time, Max,' said Derek. 'Think about it.'

'The answer is no. I don't want to spend [1] half my life sleeping in darkness. I prefer to live for a short time awake in the light. The world is a miracle and I don't want to miss any of it.' [2]

'But Dr Somaz said you will be dead before you are forty,' said Samantha, beginning to cry.

Max smiled. 'The number of years I live is not important. *How* I live is more important. What I do and what I am is more important.'

Samantha was very unhappy. 'Oh Max, my darling boy – please take the drug!'

'I'm sorry, Mum, but I can't.' Then Max smiled. 'Will you excuse me now? If I'm going to die young, I haven't got much time.'

So Max continued to work and play and live fast. But he

---

1. **spend** : (here) pass.
2. **I don't want to miss any of it** : I don't want to lose the opportunity of seeing or experiencing it.

The Boy Who Couldn't Sleep

lived a quiet, clean life. He didn't smoke or drink alcohol, and he didn't eat too much. He didn't worry about small things; [1] he didn't think about money. And he didn't waste time. He travelled a lot and looked carefully [2] at the world and people. They interested him. And he studied hard. He was always bright and awake; he always wanted to learn new things.

The medical experts said that Max's body and brain were not influenced by the diurnal rhythm, [3] like every animal on earth.

'I'm sure he's from another planet,' laughed Derek.

He liked Max's strange condition now; it was different. But Samantha didn't like it. She did everything possible to make Max normal.

For years, only a few doctors and scientists knew about Max's condition. Samantha and Derek didn't tell anybody. It was a big secret. So Max lived quietly and he was happy. When he left school, he got a job in a bank. Then he met a girl called Wendy and they fell in love and got married. Max was thirty years old. He didn't tell Wendy about his

1. **He didn't worry** [wʌri] ... **things** : he didn't let small things disturb him.
2. **carefully** : attentively.
3. **the diurnal rhythm** : the movement of day and night.

BIZARRE TALES

condition so she didn't know anything. But she began to notice things, [1] and one day she told Samantha that Max didn't sleep much but he was never tired. The two women talked, and finally Samantha told Wendy the secret.

Wendy was shocked and amazed. [2] 'Is Max really going to die before he's forty?'

'Nobody knows. Dr Somaz said that if he lives quietly, he will probably live longer. But listen, Wendy! You must not tell anybody about this — not even your friends. Nobody must know. It's a big secret.'

'Why?' said Wendy.

'Because he must live quietly. Then he will be happy and he will live longer. So the world must never know, especially the newspapers and magazines. They must never, *never* know! Do you understand, Wendy? You must never say anything to the media. [3] Promise?'

'Yes, all right, I promise,' Wendy answered.

Wendy was a good person and a good wife, but she liked money and she liked a lot of it. She loved spending money! So when she saw beautiful clothes in the shops, she was often angry because she couldn't buy them. Max didn't

---

1. **she began to notice things** : she became conscious of things.
2. **amazed** [əmeɪzd] : extremely surprised.
3. **media** [miːdiə] : newspapers, TV, etc.

The Boy Who Couldn't Sleep

get a lot of money as a bank clerk.¹ So Wendy began to think.

She thought, 'I'm going to have a child soon. If Max dies before he is forty, what will happen to us? I must think about the future.'

One day she decided to speak to Max about it. At first he was angry because she knew his secret; then he smiled.

'Wendy, my love, don't think about the future. We love each other and we are happy. That's very important! You see, nothing is certain. Perhaps I won't die young. But I promise that when I die, you will have enough ² money.'

But Wendy had a different idea. She thought about it for a few days and then she went to the office of a big national newspaper and said that she wanted to tell them an incredible story. Of course, she got thousands of pounds for the story. And when the world heard about Max, the world wanted him. America, Japan, Australia, Europe... interviews,

---

1. **bank clerk** [klɑːk] : a person who works in a bank.
2. **enough** [ɪnʌf] : sufficient.

Bizarre Tales

275 articles, talk shows, [1] documentaries... The public and the media were fascinated. [2] In a few days Max became world-famous [3] – and Wendy became very rich. He tried to hide, [4] he tried to escape from all the noise and attention. He ran away, but the media always found him.

280 Samantha knew that this was a very bad thing for Max and she was furious with Wendy. But it was too late. The TV journalists and personalities, the newspapers and magazines followed him everywhere. Film directors offered him millions of dollars to appear in their films. Big film stars 285 and rock singers wanted to meet him.

Max became unhappy; he became ill. He didn't eat and he got very thin. He lost his concentration and he stopped working hard. He also lost his interest in the world, in people, in life. He didn't want to learn new things. He locked himself [5] in his room and sat alone night and day. And Wendy continued to spend the money. One day Samantha visited him and she was

1. **talk shows** : TV programmes where famous people talk informally to an interviewer. See also 'chat show' page 64, note 3.
2. **fascinated** [fæsɪneɪtɪd] : very attracted and interested.
3. **world-famous** : famous all over the world.
4. **hide** : go where nobody could find him.
5. **locked himself** : went into his room and closed the door with a key.

The Boy Who Couldn't Sleep

shocked because he had changed a lot. He looked grey and tired. He looked old. His eyes were heavy and there were dark shadows [1] under them. Then, while Samantha was talking to him, the impossible happened: he yawned. [2] She couldn't believe her eyes.

'Are you sleepy, Max?' she asked.

'Yes. I want to sleep.'

And in a few moments he was asleep. He slept for a few hours. But when he woke up, he was still tired. A few days later he slept again. And then little by little [3] he began to sleep like a normal person.

'You sleep eight hours a day now, Max,' Samantha said, frightened. 'What's happening to you?'

'I don't know,' he replied. 'I feel tired. I need to sleep.'

'But why?'

'Because I don't want to stay awake now. The world is boring; people are boring. It's better to sleep.'

When he fell asleep quickly, Samantha went home. She was very anxious and very unhappy. Now Max was beginning to sleep more than a normal person! He had no more bright energy, no more interest in life. He just seemed very tired.

Now the public and the media were completely obsessed

---

1. **shadows** [ʃædəʊz] : (here) dark areas on the skin under the eyes.
2. **yawned** [jɔːnd] : opened his mouth wide and took in air because he was sleepy.
3. **little by little** : gradually.

Bizarre Tales

with Max. Photographers [1] stood outside his house all day and night and took photos of Max when he yawned and when he was asleep. Every day Wendy told reporters what Max was doing – for a fee, [2] of course. All round the world people knew what Max was doing every minute of the day. They tried to telephone him, they sent letters, telegrams and presents.

Samantha said to herself, 'If this continues, Max will die. It must stop.'

She thought about it day and night. And then one day she decided to appear on a TV chat show. [3]

'He's very ill,' she said in the studio. 'You must all leave him alone.'

'Why is he ill?' the interviewer asked. 'Is the drug killing him?'

'No, he doesn't take any drugs!' said Samantha angrily. 'It's *you* – the newspaper and TV people – and *you* – the public! You have destroyed his peace and his world with all

---

1. **Photographers** [fəˈtɒgrəfəz] : people who take photographs as a profession.
2. **fee** : (here) money paid for information.
3. **chat show** : see 'talk shows' page 62, note 1.

The Boy Who Couldn't Sleep

your noise and gossip.[1] You won't let him live quietly. He always lived in the light with his eyes open but you have pulled him down into your darkness and he has closed his eyes. You – the media and the public – are killing Max with your stupidity. Leave him alone!'

The media and the public were very angry. Next day there was a lot of anger about it on TV and in the newspapers.

'Us?' one newspaper article began. 'Is Max Price's mother accusing us? Yes, she is saying that *we* – the people and the press [2] – are destroying her son. But isn't he rich now? And isn't he famous? Hasn't Mrs Price asked herself who made him rich and famous? We are innocent, Mrs Price. We have helped your son. You told us to leave him alone. But we live in a democracy. We have a right to [3] know about Max Price. We demand [4] to know about him!...'

Etcetera, etcetera.

When Samantha left the TV studio, she went to Max's house. Wendy told her that he was sleeping so she went home. Next day Wendy phoned Samantha.

'I'm frightened,' she said. 'Max is still sleeping. Please come!'

---

1. **gossip** : talk about other people.
2. **the press** : newspapers and magazines.
3. **we have a right to** : it is our civil privilege to.
4. **demand** : ask in a very strong way.

Bizarre Tales

When Samantha arrived, there were reporters [1] and photographers and two TV cameras outside the house. She pushed her way to the door and went in. Wendy was sitting on the sofa. She looked terrified.

'Why doesn't he wake up?' she cried.

The women went upstairs to Max's room. He was in bed. His eyes were closed; his face was very pale. [2] Samantha touched him.

'He's very cold,' she said. 'Call Dr Somaz.'

Dr Somaz came and began to examine Max. Just then Derek arrived.

'There's a very big crowd outside,' he said.

Then he saw that the women were crying. He looked at Dr Somaz, who said to him:

'Tell the people to go away. Max is dead.'

Next day Max's death was big news all over the world. The newspapers, the magazines, and the TV news all had the same opinion.

'The boy who couldn't sleep has finally found eternal rest. As the doctors always said, he died before he was forty. This shows that the people and the media are not responsible.'

---

1. **reporters** : people who report news for newspapers or TV. Also journalists.
2. **pale** [peɪl] : without much colour, white.

ACTIVITIES

After reading

1 Complete this summary of the story. Fill in the blanks or underline the appropriate word.

When Max Price was a baby, he didn't sleep much ¹(and/because) his mother Samantha thought he was intelligent. ²(So/But) a psychologist told her that a ³...................... of modern ⁴...................... were like Max.

When he was five, he ⁵(played/slept) for only two hours a night. And in his teens he was ⁶.......................... for twenty-three hours a ⁷.......................... . He told his friends that people slept too ⁸(little/much).

Samantha was ⁹(anxious/happy) about his condition. She tried putting ¹⁰.......................... tablets in his tea. ¹¹(But/Then) she wrote to an expert on sleep, who said that Max's brain waves were ¹².......................... . He also said it was possible that Max would die ¹³(before/after) he was forty, although he thought that Max would probably live longer ¹⁴(but/if) he took a ¹⁵.......................... . Max said ¹⁶.......................... .

After that, Max continued to live fast, but his life was clean and ¹⁷.......................... . He studied hard and learnt a lot of things about the ¹⁸(world/life) and people. Then he got married. When his wife Wendy learnt about his condition, she was shocked. She liked money very much and she began to think about the ¹⁹.......................... . She decided to ²⁰(buy/sell) Max's story to a ²¹.......................... and get lots of money.

Then Max became ²².......................... all over the world. He tried to ²³(hide/live) from the media but it was impossible. ²⁴(When/So) he became ill and he lost ²⁵.......................... in life. When he began to sleep like normal people, the public and the media became ²⁶(obsessed/angry) with him. Samantha said on TV that they were destroying Max and next day they were very ²⁷(obssessed/angry). On that day Max ²⁸.......................... . Afterwards, the media said that they were not ²⁹(responsible/innocent).

ACTIVITIES

2 Who do these sentences refer to? Write S (Samantha), D (Derek), P (the psychologist), Ds (the doctors), W (Wendy), M (Max), Sz (Dr Somaz), or PM (the public and the media). Sometimes you must write the letters in more than one box.

Who...

a. ☐ liked money?
b. ☐ thought that Max didn't sleep because he was intelligent?
c. ☐ said that five-year-old Max was a hyper-active child?
d. ☐ slept very little as a baby?
e. ☐ accepted Max's condition?
f. ☐ said that Max's case wasn't strange because modern babies slept less?
g. ☐ did some tests on Max?
h. ☐ were obsessed with Max?
i. ☐ told the media to leave Max alone?
j. ☐ said that Max's brain waves were different?
k. ☐ became rich and spent a lot of money?
l. ☐ told Samantha that Max was genetically different from them?

ACTIVITIES

3 **A.** The verbs in the alarm clock are all in the infinitive form. Indicate them with a clock hand, like the example. Then write them in the 'infinitive' column of the table and complete the 'Past irregular' column.

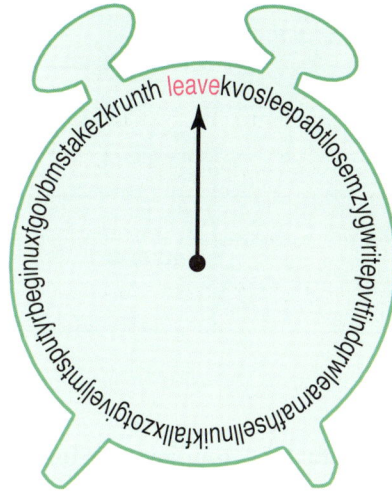

Infinitive	Past irregular
leave	left

B. Now complete the sentences with some of the verbs in 3A. Use the Past tense!

a. When he was five, Max never .... asleep before eleven o'clock.

b. Max .... away from all the noise and attention but the media always .... him.

c. Baby Max .... all day, like other babies.

d. Samantha .... a letter to a famous neurologist.

e. Wendy .... to a newspaper office and .... the story of Max for thousands of pounds.

f. Max stopped working hard and he .... his interest in the world.

ACTIVITIES

4 A. Complete the table with the comparative (-er) form of the adjectives. Then write the opposites and their comparative forms.

Adjective	Comparative	Opposite	Comparative
early			
fast			
bright		dark	
young			
short			
noisy			quieter
interesting	more interesting		

B. Now complete the sentences with the comparative form of some of the adjectives in 4A.

a. Max looks .... than eighteen. He looks about thirty-five.
b. Max died before he was forty; his life was .... than normal.
c. In the past people went to bed ....
d. Electric light is .... than candlelight.
e. The modern world is fast and noisy. Life was .... and .... in the past.

ACTIVITIES

5 Match the sentences in A with their endings in B.

A

a. If Max takes the drug for a long time,

b. Max will live longer

c. If the brain is always awake,

d. Wendy is thinking about what will happen to her

e. Max will die

B

1. if Max dies before he is forty.

2. the body will get old quickly.

3. it will kill him in the end.

4. if the media doesn't leave him alone.

5. if he lives quietly.

6 Complete the dialogue with the words in the box.

sleepy   awake   asleep   sleeping   sleep (x 2)

Max: How did I fall ¹............................ ?

Samantha: I put some ²............................ tablets in your tea.

Max: You must never do that again, Mum!

Samantha: But ³............................ restores the body, Max. If you don't sleep, you'll die.

Max: I don't need ⁴............................ , Mum. I want to stay ⁵............................ . I want to live with my eyes open.
(Max yawns)

Samantha: Do you feel ⁶............................ , Max?

Max: Yes. I want to sleep.

ACTIVITIES

7 Listen to lines 44-82. Then, without looking at the text, put the sentences in the correct part of the table. Write a, b, c, etc.

Five years old	
Eight years old	
Teenager	

a. He slept about two hours a night.
b. He went to bed at about 9.30 pm.
c. He went to discos and parties.
d. He worked hard at school.
e. The doctors said that he was hyper-active.
f. He woke up between 4-5 a.m.
g. He thought that sleep was a waste of time.
h. He played with his toys at night.
i. Derek said that Max was Nature's experiment.
j. He read a lot of books.

Now listen again and check your answers.

ACTIVITIES

8 **A.** Do you agree with these statements? Write a few words about them.

- We don't like the night and we don't want to sleep.
- He (Max) is a child of the future.
- We sleep too much. Sleep is a waste of time.
- The number of years we live is not important. *How* we live is more important.

B. Did you like the end of the story? Say why/why not? Do you want to change it? Write your own ending.

ACTIVITIES

Before reading

1 What do you associate with each season of the year?

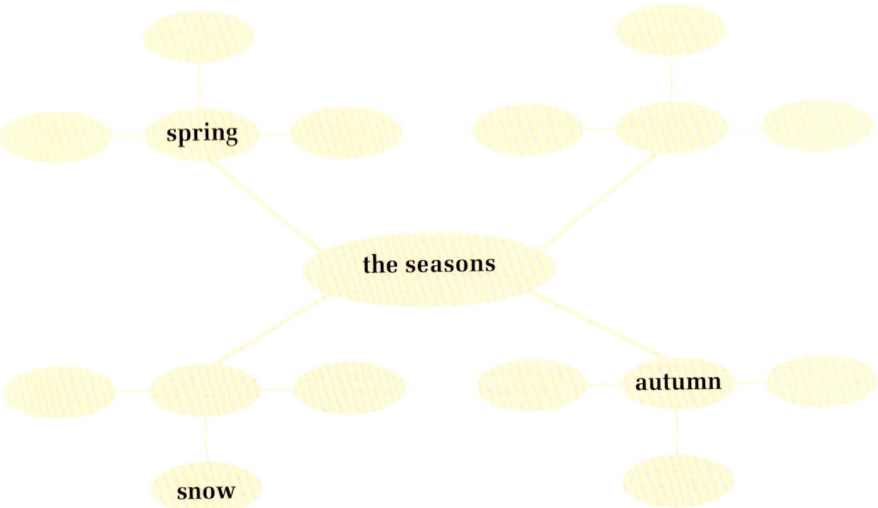

2 Find 10 words for clothes or parts of the body in the word puzzle. Then write them in the correct column in the table. One has been done for you.

X	L	E	G	S	U	J	H	V	W
N	Z	B	M	Y	P	X	A	L	S
T	I	G	H	T	S	R	N	Q	O
Z	C	J	E	F	A	Z	D	I	C
T	R	O	U	S	E	R	S	B	K
U	F	V	X	H	N	L	W	X	S
F	C	H	O	E	G	V	K	P	Q
E	H	A	K	A	S	H	O	E	S
E	N	T	Y	D	M	K	D	T	P
T	Y	Z	O	G	L	O	V	E	S

Clothes	Parts of body
tights	

Fiona's Spring Dress

That evening hundreds of eyes were watching Fiona as she walked along the catwalk. [1] All the important names in the fashion and media world were there: designers, journalists, singers, film stars and TV celebrities. [2] But Fiona was a famous fashion model [3] so she didn't feel afraid or embarrassed; in fact, she enjoyed all the attention. But

---

1. **catwalk** : long, narrow platform where people walk to exhibit clothes.
2. **TV celebrities** [sɪˈlebrɪtɪz] : people famous on TV.
3. **model** : a person who shows clothes as a profession by wearing them.

Bizarre Tales

tonight she felt angry and unhappy again and she didn't know why.

It wasn't the clothes she was wearing. They showed a lot of her body but Fiona didn't feel shy about this. To be a model you have to be an exhibitionist.[1] And anyway Fiona got a lot of money for her work. So why did she have these strange feelings again? Why did she feel so angry with all the people at the fashion show?

As she was going to turn round at the end of the catwalk something mysterious and horrifying[2] happened.

Afterwards everyone had his or her ideas about what happened. Some people thought that it was a spark[3] from an electric cable.[4] Others said that Fiona's dress was inflammable and perhaps a spark from a cigarette flew[5] on to it.

There weren't any flames. Fiona's dress just started to burn. It became brown at the bottom and began to curl up,[6] like a piece of paper. It didn't really catch fire; it began to smoulder[7] like a cigarette. Fiona saw the smoke and screamed.

1. **exhibitionist** : a person who likes to attract attention to him/herself.
2. **horrifying** [hɒ'rɪfaɪɪŋ] : causing horror or shock.
3. **spark** : a small, very hot particle (of electricity or fire).
4. **cable** [keɪbəl] : a long, thick piece of wire for carrying electricity.
5. **flew** [fluː] : moved through the air. The past of the verb 'to fly'.
6. **curl** [kɜːl] **up** : (here) bend upwards from the heat of fire.
7. **smoulder** [sməʊldə] : burn slowly.

Bizarre Tales

'Her dress is burning!' shouted someone.

'Oh, my beautiful dress, my poor beautiful dress!' This was Byron Gagliano, the dress designer.

Fiona was very frightened. She ran back along the catwalk, screaming. Then somebody jumped on to the catwalk and poured a bottle of mineral water over her. The dress stopped burning. Fiona ran behind some curtains [1] and fainted. [2]

She woke up in a hospital bed. The room was full of flowers and fruit and chocolates and get-well cards. [3] The first thing she saw when she opened her eyes was a smiling mouth full of big white teeth. Byron Gagliano was sitting by her bed.

'Hallo, darling. How are you feeling?' he said.

'Why am I here? What's happening?'

'It's okay, Fiona. The doctor said you're going to be fine.'

She looked at him with terrified [4] eyes. 'Am I badly burnt?'

---

1. **curtains** [kɜːtənz] : long pieces of material, usually for covering windows.
2. **fainted** : lost consciousness for a brief time.
3. **get-well cards** : illustrated cards that we send to people when they are ill.
4. **terrified** : very frightened.

Fiona's Spring Dress

'No. Your legs are a bit red, like sunburn. [1] Nothing serious, sweetie. Relax.'

'How long have I been here?'

'All night. They had to give you a sedative. But you're okay now, baby. [2] Here – have a grape. [3] They're delicious!'

But Fiona didn't want a grape; she wanted to go home.

'You can't,' said Byron. 'The doc says you have to stay here and rest. You've had a bit of a shock. He wants to ask you some questions. He wants to know what happened. Well, honey? Do you know what happened?'

'No...' Fiona began, with tears in her eyes. 'I came out on to the catwalk and...'

'Go on,' said Byron, his mouth full of chocolate.

'And I felt very angry.'

'Why?'

'Oh – all those stupid people... looking at me...'

Byron looked surprised.

'Well, I don't know if they are stupid but they're certainly

---

1. **sunburn** [sʌˌnbɜːn] : inflammation of the skin caused by the sun.
2. **baby** : (American slang) usually, it is used for a man's girlfriend, but here Byron is only expressing affection for Fiona. He also calls her 'honey', 'sweetheart', 'sweetie', and 'darling' in the same way.
3. **grape** [ɡreɪp] : green or red fruit used for making wine.

BiZArrE TaLeS

rich! They pay a lot of money for my clothes. You mustn't be
angry, sweetheart. You're a model. It's your job.'

'But...'

'But what, Fiona? Where's the problem? They'll buy anything if it's in fashion. But they're our customers. We need them.'

'Oh, please listen! It's important that now I'm beginning to understand why I was angry with those people.'

'But you haven't explained why your dress started to burn.'

'Well, you see, I've felt angry and unhappy before and nothing happened. But last night it was very, very strong – stronger than before.'

Byron shook his head. 'What are you saying? Are you serious, baby?'

'Yes. You see, last night on the catwalk I felt that something inside me was trying to get out. [1] It was a strong burning feeling.'

Byron looked at her with his mouth open. Then he popped [2] another chocolate into it. Fiona continued.

1. **get out** : escape.
2. **popped** : put quickly.

Fiona's Spring Dress

'I understood that people at fashion shows only look at the clothes I'm wearing – or my body. They never see the real me, the invisible me inside.'

'The invisible you!' Byron stopped eating in amazement.[1] 'What are you talking about?'

'Last night the part of me that people never see was burning to get out. That's why my dress started to burn.'

'Stop, stop!' Byron shouted, his face red with anger. 'Fiona darling, you're a fashion model! You model clothes – visible things.'

'Well, there's an invisible part of me and I want people to see that.'

'But how can they if it's invisible?'

Fiona was silent for a moment. Then she said, 'I don't know.'

'Right, sweetie. You don't know because it's impossible. You haven't got an invisible part. Fashion models haven't got invisible parts.'

'That's why I'm going to stop modelling.'

Byron looked really shocked. 'You mean... ?'

'Yes! I'm going to look for another career.'

Now Byron's face was as white as his teeth. 'Fiona! No! You're the best model in the world. Think of me. What will I

---

1. **amazement** : great surprise.

Bizarre Tales

do? Who will sell my clothes? People buy them because they
want to look as beautiful as *you*. Please, Fiona, don't scare
me! What will happen to my spring collection?' [1]

He looked very frightened. He was nearly crying. For a
while Fiona didn't say anything. She smiled at Byron. She
was thinking.

'All right, I'll model your spring collection,' she said.
'But only if I can show the hidden [2] part of me.'

'But why, darling?' Byron said timidly. 'Who wants to
buy that?'

'You just said that they would buy anything if it's in
fashion.'

Byron began to eat an apple. He didn't know what to say.
This was a very different Fiona. Then he said:

'If you think people want to see the real you, you're
making a big mistake. Fashion is not about reality; it's about
fantasy. People see what they want to see.'

'Well, I'll make them see the real me. I'm going to give
them a big shock.'

'How?'

'Wait and see,' Fiona answered with a wicked [3] smile.

Byron didn't like that smile; it frightened him.

---

1. **spring collection** : clothes designed specially for spring.
2. **hidden** : not visible. The past of the verb 'to hide'.
3. **wicked** [wɪkɪd] : (here) naughty, or malicious.

Fiona's Spring Dress

'What are you going to do, Fiona?'

'I told you. I'm going to show them the hidden me: the real woman, not the superficial model.'

'But what *is* the real, hidden you, baby?'

'I don't know, but I've changed, Byron. I'm not a model now. I'm not a doll [1] that you designers dress up. I'm a real woman and I've got a soul.' [2]

'What's that?' Byron asked, peeling a banana.

Fiona tried to smile. 'It's the part of you that other people don't know. It's secret and private. It likes to stay in the dark because it's shy and quiet. But it's the only thing that's true about you. It doesn't change like fashion. It's always the same – the true you.'

'Oh God, you *have* changed, darling!' Byron said unhappily. 'You've never spoken like this before.'

'Maybe because I've found my soul and it's speaking for the first time.'

'Really? But how did you lose it, sweetie?'

'I sold it, Byron. But I've got it back.'

---

1. **doll** : a child's small model of a human being.
2. **soul** [səʊl] : the spiritual part of a person.

Bizarre Tales

'Oh well, I must go now, honey,' Byron said impatiently, kissing her cheek. 'I've got so much work. The spring collection comes out next month. Look, Fiona, you're a wonderful model – the best! Forget about your soul. Come and sell my clothes for me.'

The spring collection was at the end of March. Byron worked very hard. He made clothes with spring colours – yellows and greens – and spring designs: lots of leaves and blossom,[1] flowers, birds, and even eggs.

There were clothes with soft feathers[2] – like the feathers of chicks or ducklings – and clothes made of lambswool too.

Byron called it the Pasqua Collection and it was shown in London. The fashion and media people came in flocks[3] like sheep. The whole show was really funny, but everybody was serious about it. They knew it was all about money. You could smell it in the air.

Byron wanted a 'cultural' fashion show. He knew that culture could sell his clothes because the snobs liked it. So

---

1. **blossom** : (here) flowers that grow on trees.
2. **feathers** [feðəz] :
3. **flocks** : a lot of sheep or birds together.

Fiona's Spring Dress

there wasn't any of the usual loud, monotonous music; only the sounds of spring, poetry and classical music. They played [1] the part of Beethoven's pastoral symphony with the call of a cuckoo. [2] Then there was a poem: 'Oh, to be in England, now that April's here!' The people liked all this because it made them feel intelligent.

Some models were dressed in cuckoo grey; others had swallows' wings for sleeves. [3] One model came out of a big plastic egg. Another one hopped [4] along the catwalk like a bunny [5] rabbit. She wore a cap with rabbit's ears and she had a little round tail behind. Another model, dressed in white wool with a lamb's tail, danced around like a lamb in spring. The people laughed and clapped at these funny things. But they were waiting for the big attraction of the evening. The catalogue said:

'Top model Fiona Sharp

1. **played** : (here) caused a cassette or CD to produce music.
2. **cuckoo** [kʊkuː] : bird with a call like its name, usually associated with spring.
3. **sleeves** : parts of a coat, shirt, etc. that cover the arms.
4. **hopped** : moved with small jumps – like a frog, for example!
5. **bunny** : a child's word for rabbit.

Bizarre Tales

concludes the evening with a very special Gagliano creation which represents spring waking up from the sleep of winter.'

Byron had designed a long, white robe [1] with a hood. [2] This was winter. Under it Fiona wore a creation of bright sun-yellow and spring green, which shone like a beautiful spring day. Fiona had to lie [3] on the catwalk like a sleeping person. Then the curtains would open to the music of Stravinsky's 'Rite of Spring'. This music begins quietly, then suddenly it becomes loud and dramatic. Fiona had to wake up, throw off the white robe of winter, and reveal [4] the spring dress.

At first everything went well. When the lights went down, the curtains opened slowly. Fiona was lying [5] on the catwalk like a sleeping ghost. The music was quiet, but strange and frightening, like the music in a horror film. The people waited in silence, but they were very excited. Then

---

1. **robe** [rəʊb] : a long coat made from one piece of material and without buttons.
2. **hood** [hʊd] : part of a jacket or coat that covers the head.
3. **lie** [laɪ] : to put her body horizontally on the floor of the catwalk.
4. **reveal** [rɪˈviːl] : show, let people see.
5. **lying** [laɪɪŋ] : participle of the verb 'to lie'. See note 3.

Fiona's Spring Dress

the music suddenly changed and Fiona woke up and took off the robe. But she wasn't wearing the spring dress. In fact, she wasn't wearing anything. She was completely naked. [1]

Behind the curtains Byron put his hands over his eyes.

'Oh no, this is terrible!' he said to himself. 'Fiona, what are you doing to me? Everybody is going to laugh at me!'

But nobody laughed. There was a deep silence. Byron opened the curtains a little and looked. Fiona was dancing to the music. It was a strange dance. It wasn't modern; it was an old, primitive kind of dance. Perhaps it was thousands of years old. It was the kind of dance that very ancient people did to celebrate spring. It wasn't personal or individual like modern dancing; it was wild [2] and violent like a storm. It didn't look like human dancing; there was something savage and animal about it.

Byron couldn't believe his eyes. What was Fiona doing? Her face had a strange look. She seemed hypnotised. She moved her body like a puppet [3] on strings.

Byron couldn't understand. Was she crazy? Then he remembered Fiona's words: 'I'm going to show them the real me.' Did this dance express the real Fiona? Was she really so wild? Now she was showing her teeth, like an angry dog.

---

1. **naked** [neɪkɪd] : not wearing clothes, nude.
2. **wild** : (here) undisciplined, without control.
3. **puppet** : a kind of doll that moves on strings.

Bizarre Tales

Her eyes were yellow and fierce [1] like a wild cat's. Her long blonde hair flew round her face like flames in the wind.

This isn't Fiona, thought Byron. It's a wild woman.

He thought that she was going to jump into the audience [2] and attack the people with her teeth. Frightened, he ran from behind the curtains. Then he stopped on the catwalk. The people didn't look surprised or shocked or angry. They seemed to think that nothing strange was happening. They were talking and smiling as usual. Byron was very surprised. He jumped off the catwalk.

'Congratulations, Mr Gagliano!' said a woman – a famous actress – 'Your dress is a masterpiece!' [3]

Byron looked at her with his mouth open. Then he looked at Fiona and he was sure that she wasn't wearing any clothes. He looked at the actress again. Was she joking? He turned to the other people. Another woman was saying to her friend:

'It's a wonderful dress! Don't you think so, Justine?'

'Oh yes – it's really wonderful!' replied her companion. And she pointed at Fiona with her pen. 'It's got the shape of

---

1. **fierce** [fɪəs] : intense and aggressive.
2. **audience** [ɔːdɪəns] : people who watch or listen to something (a play, a concert, TV, etc.).
3. **masterpiece** [mɑːstəpiːs] : a person's best piece of work, usually an artist or writer.

Fiona's Spring Dress

crocuses and daffodils [1] just before they come out. And the colours are so fresh and delicate, like spring blossom...'

Byron turned to look at Fiona again. He looked and looked but he couldn't see any dress. Are they all crazy, he thought? Or am *I* crazy? Or perhaps I'm dreaming. The strange music was loud in his ears, and Fiona was dancing in a frenzy. [2] Byron thought: Yes, I *am* dreaming. It's all a crazy dream!

But then the people started to clap and cheer. [3]

Some of them stood up; and then everybody stood up.

'Bravo!... Brilliant!... Superb!... Fabulous!... Fantastic!'

Byron heard these words and he saw that the people were all looking at him with big smiles.

'That creation is a work of genius!' said a very important person.

Byron's head was going round and round. 'What creation?' he asked.

---

1. **crocuses** [krəʊkəsɪz] **and daffodils** [dæfədɪlz] : spring flowers.
2. **frenzy** : a state of violent excitement.
3. **clap and cheer** : hit their hands together and shout with pleasure or encouragement.

Bizarre Tales

'The dress of course! It's the greatest thing in the fashion world!'

'Well, thank you,' Byron said.

And when he looked at Fiona again, he suddenly understood. These people are seeing what they want to see, he thought. They don't want to see the hidden Fiona; they want to see her in a beautiful dress, and that's what they can see. Fashion is fantasy, not reality. They'll never see reality because they don't want to. They like only visible things. Ha! Ha! I told Fiona she was making a big mistake...'

And Byron began to laugh... and laugh... and laugh...

After reading

1 Tick the correct answer.

   a. When Fiona walked along the catwalk, she felt
   ☐ angry and unhappy.
   ☐ afraid and embarrassed.
   ☐ shy and strange.

   b. What happened on the catwalk?
   ☐ A spark fell on Fiona's dress.
   ☐ Fiona caught fire.
   ☐ Fiona's dress started to burn.

   c. When she woke up, she was
   ☐ badly burnt.
   ☐ at the doctor's.
   ☐ terrified.

   d. As she talked to Byron, Fiona
   ☐ began to understand why her dress had started to burn.
   ☐ began to eat fruit and chocolate.
   ☐ began to feel angry.

   e. Fiona said that her dress started to burn because
   ☐ a lot of eyes were watching her.
   ☐ something inside her was trying to get out.
   ☐ she was unhappy.

   f. Byron didn't believe
   ☐ that people only wanted to look at Fiona's clothes and body.
   ☐ that Fiona had an invisible part.
   ☐ that Fiona's dress started to burn.

ACTIVITIES

g. Why was Byron frightened when Fiona said she wanted to stop modelling?
- [ ] He was thinking about his fashion business.
- [ ] He was thinking about Fiona's future.
- [ ] He was thinking about Fiona's wicked smile.

h. Fiona said that at the spring show she
- [ ] wasn't going to model Byron's collection.
- [ ] was going to show people what they wanted to see.
- [ ] was going to shock people.

i. Fiona said, 'I've got a soul.' Did Byron understand this?
- [ ] Yes, but he didn't want to admit it.
- [ ] No.
- [ ] Don't know.

j. Byron's fashion show was
- [ ] intelligent and cultured.
- [ ] about money.
- [ ] in the morning.

k. When Fiona took off the robe, she was wearing
- [ ] a green and yellow dress.
- [ ] nothing.
- [ ] winter clothes.

l. The people
- [ ] thought Fiona was wearing a dress.
- [ ] were surprised.
- [ ] stopped talking.

m. What did Byron suddenly understand?
- [ ] That the people were crazy.
- [ ] That the dress was a masterpiece.
- [ ] That the people didn't want to see reality.

ACTIVITIES

2 Write a few sentences about the most important things that happened at these places:

the catwalk
....

the hospital
....

the fashion show
....

3 Circle the word that is different from the others and write the correct category, like the example.

a. journalist   designer   doctor   (cigarette)   ..professions..
b. teeth   eyes   spark   mouth   ....
c. bottle   dress   cap   robe   ....
d. actress   grape   apple   banana   ....
e. red   poetry   green   yellow   ....
f. spring   summer   autumn   night   ....
g. March   July   Friday   October   ....
h. duck   bed   chicken   cuckoo   ....
i. rose   daffodil   model   crocus   ....
j. rabbit   cat   sheep   dog   ....

> seasons   birds   ~~professions~~   months
> pets   parts of the body
> fruit   clothes   colours   flowers

ACTIVITIES

4 Read lines 163-92 and tick the things that are mentioned.

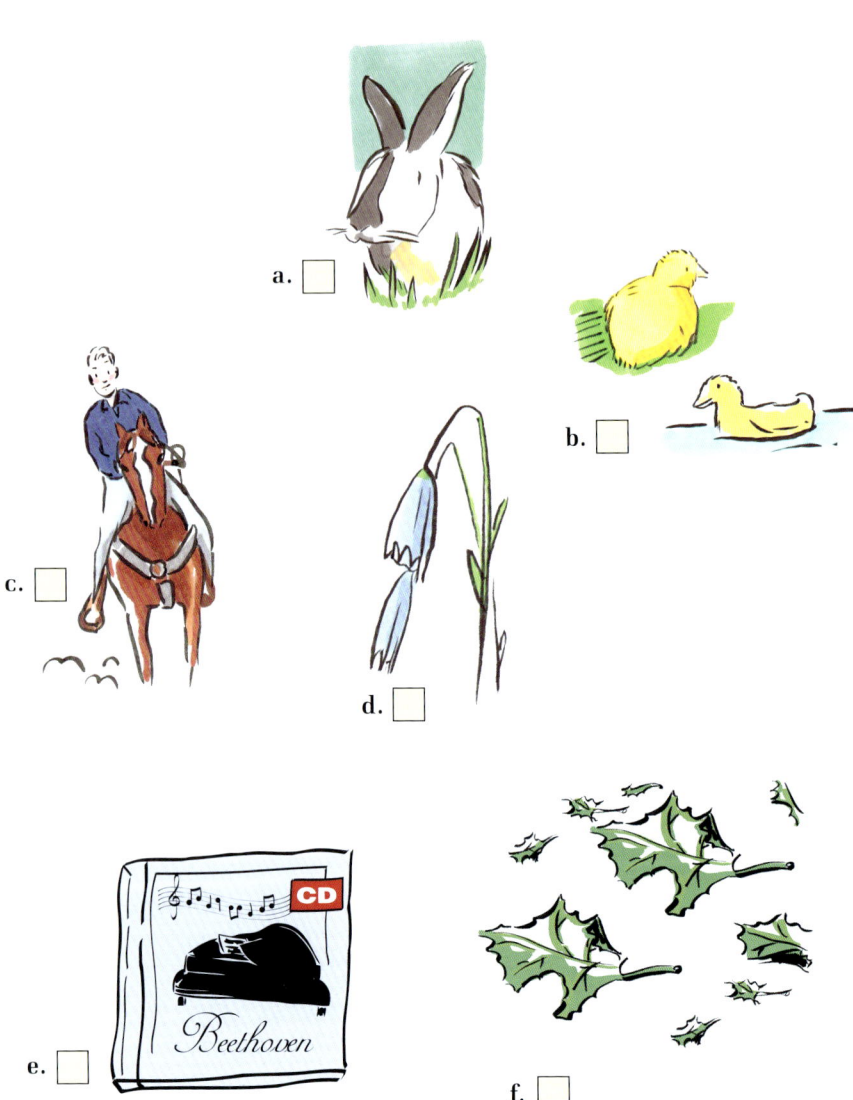

a.

b.

c.

d.

e.

f.

ACTIVITIES

5 **A.** Which adjectives refer to the words on the right? Match the numbers to the adjectives, like the example. An adjective may have more than one number.

2	wild	1. Byron's spring fashion show
	private	2. Fiona's dance
	stupid	3. Byron's customers
	frightened	4. Fiona on the catwalk
	mysterious	5. Byron when Fiona said she was going to stop modelling
	violent	
	unhappy	6. What happened on the catwalk
	rich	7. Fiona's soul
	shocked	
	angry	
	quiet	
	funny	
	primitive	

B. Now complete the sentences with some of the adjectives from 5A.

a. When Fiona turned round on the catwalk, something .... happened.
b. Fiona's dance was .... and ...., like a storm.
c. Byron was .... and .... when Fiona told him she was going to stop modelling.
d. Byron's customers are .... but ....

ACTIVITIES

6 First complete the questions with do, does, was (x2), were (x2), did (x3), has, have. Then complete the answers, like the example.

a. .... Fiona feel angry and unhappy on the catwalk?
Yes, she did.

b. .... Fiona want a grape?
No,

c. .... the people surprised about Fiona's dance?
....

d. .... Fiona changed?
....

e. .... Byron frightened when Fiona said she was going to stop modelling?
....

f. .... Fiona's dress start to burn?
....

g. .... Byron's teeth big and white?
....

h. In Byron's opinion, ... fashion models got souls?
....

i. .... the customers pay a lot of money for Byron's clothes?
....

j. .... Fiona wearing a spring dress?
....

k. .... Byron need his customers?
....

ACTIVITIES

7 **Answer these questions.**

   a. 'Fashion is fantasy.' Do you agree with Byron?
   Yes? Give your reasons.   No, Why not?

   b. What did the story seem to say about the *real* Fiona? Choose from the words below.
   The real Fiona was

   ☐ old   ☐ savage   ☐ angry   ☐ crazy   ☐ wild
   ☐ violent   ☐ primitive   ☐ barbaric   ☐ fierce   ☐ happy

   Were you surprised about the real Fiona?
   Yes? Why?   No? Why not?

ACTIVITIES

Before reading

1 Answer the questionnaire about your life-style. You can tick (✓) more than one box.

a. What is your usual diet?
- [ ] a lot of fast food
- [ ] a lot of fresh fruit & vegetables
- [ ] a lot of meat & pasta

b. Do you do any of these regularly?
- [ ] smoke
- [ ] drink alcohol
- [ ] eat a lot of sweets and chocolate

c. How do you usually go to school?
- [ ] walk
- [ ] cycle
- [ ] by car, motorbike, etc.

d. What do you usually do in your free time?
- [ ] watch TV/videos
- [ ] play sports
- [ ] play computer games

e. What other things do you do for entertainment?
- [ ] go to discos
- [ ] read books
- [ ] listen to music

f. Do you think your life-style is healthy?
- [ ] yes
- [ ] no
- [ ] don't know

2 Write a few things that you like or dislike about living in the twentieth century.

Examples: high crime rate, rock music

I like ....

....

....

I dislike ....

....

....

A Twentieth-Century Malady

He looked a sad young man and we wanted to be kind to him. When he moved into [1] the house next to ours, my wife Janet said, 'I think he's sad because he lives alone. [2] I feel sorry for him.' [3]

We live in a semi-detached [4] house outside a village. The house next to ours was empty for a long time, and then the young man came. He arrived in a van [5] with a few pieces of

---

1. **moved into** : came to live in.
2. **alone** : without a companion.
3. **I feel sorry for him** : I feel sympathy and concern for his situation.
4. **semi-detached** [semidɪtætʃt] **house** : one of two houses that have a common wall.
5. **van** : vehicle for transporting various things.

Bizarre Tales

furniture.[1] Then we didn't see him very much. Sometimes he went for a walk in the country. And every day he walked to
the village to do some shopping. He always walked; he didn't have a car.

'Perhaps he's too poor to buy a car,' said Janet. 'Let's take him into the village tomorrow.'

So next day when he came out of the house to go shopping, I offered him a lift.[2]

'No, thank you,' he replied. 'I prefer to walk.'

We looked surprised. 'But it's over[3] a mile to the village,' I said.

He smiled. 'I like walking.' And he walked on.

'He's just shy, poor boy,' Janet said.

So we tried again. Next time he came out, we were waiting in the car. We said that we were going to the village and offered

---

1. **furniture** [fɜːnɪtʃə] : table, chair, bed, etc.
2. **a lift** (here) a free ride in a car, etc.
3. **over** : (here) more than.

A Twentieth-Century Malady

him a lift. He looked away quickly. Was he angry or shy?

'Thank you very much but I prefer to walk,' he said. And he walked on.

Janet was surprised. But she continued to think about how to help the young man.

'He's very thin,' she said one evening. 'I'm sure he doesn't eat good food. We must invite him to dinner.'

Janet and I like good food. We eat a lot of butter and puddings [1] and cream and sweet things like cakes. We know this rich [2] food is fattening [3] but we like it. So we're a bit overweight. [4]

The young man opened the door. Janet was right: he was thin. I invited him to dinner. He looked at me in silence a moment and smiled.

'Thank you. You're very kind but I can only eat certain food. I have a special diet.'

'What sort of diet?'

'Oh fruit, vegetables, bread...'

'Are you a vegetarian?'

'Yes, I am.'

'My wife is a very good cook,' I said. 'She can cook a

---

1. **puddings** : desserts.
2. **rich** : (here) with a lot of fat, eggs, butter, or spices.
3. **fattening** : causing fat in the body.
4. **overweight** [əʊvə'weɪt] : weighing more than normal.

BiZArrE TaLeS

50 delicious vegetarian dinner. Please come.'

He looked away and said nothing.

'You must come,' I insisted. 'My wife will be very disappointed.' [1]

He thought a moment. 'Okay, I'll come,' he said. He
55 didn't look very happy about it.

But Janet was very happy. She cooked a wonderful vegetarian meal. But she put butter in the vegetables. And she also made a big fruit pudding with lots of sugar and cream.

60 'He *must* eat some real food,' she said.

That evening we learnt the young man's name: Richard. He didn't talk much but we also learnt that he was twenty-eight. He couldn't find a job and he didn't have much money. His parents were dead and he didn't have any
65 brothers or sisters. We felt sorry for him.

He didn't eat much that evening. He said he wasn't hungry. Janet was a little offended.

'I cooked all that horrible vegetarian food for him and he left it on his plate. And he didn't drink any wine, either!' [2]

70 Yes, Janet was a bit angry. But she quickly forgot about it. Then she began to think about Richard again.

---

1. **disappointed** [dɪsəpɔɪntɪd] : sad.
2. **either!** [aɪðə] : too or also with a negative.

Bizarre Tales

'Poor boy! He's all alone in that house,' she said. 'He hasn't got any friends and he hasn't got a girlfriend. It's terrible! What does he do all evening?' She looked at me sadly.

'He watches telly, like us.'

Suddenly she had an idea. 'We must invite him to come and watch telly with us! That will cheer him up!' [1]

'I think he likes to be alone, Janet,' I said. 'He's a quiet person.'

'But he isn't happy. I can see it.'

'How? He doesn't speak or laugh much, but I think he's happy.'

'Well, I say he *isn't* happy, Reg. You must go and bring him here this evening. I want him to be happy!'

So I went out into the cold, wet night and knocked on Richard's door.

'Would you like to come round to us?' I asked.

He smiled. 'Why?'

'Oh – we can watch telly and have a bit of food.'

He suddenly looked frightened. 'No! Not telly! I never watch it.' His face was very white.

Now I was really surprised. 'Well – perhaps you want some company...'

---

1. **cheer him up!** : make him happy.

A Twentieth-Century Malady

'I like my own company,' he said. And he shut the door quickly.

When I told Janet, she was furious. 'Who does he think he is? We only want to be kind to him.'

At three o'clock the next morning she woke me up.

'Hey, Reg! Wake up! I've got a great idea!' she cried, a big, happy smile on her face. 'We'll have a big party with all our friends and relatives. We'll tell Richard that there will be a lot of noise and invite him to come.'

I didn't like the idea. '*I'm* not going to invite him this time. Goodnight, dear!'

So Janet invited Richard to the party. He couldn't say no, poor boy! But Janet told him he had to[1] come and he came. But I could see he wasn't happy. There was loud music and dancing, lots of delicious fattening food, cigarette smoke, and bottles and bottles of alcoholic drink. Our friends and relatives are all very kind and they pushed plates of food and glasses of drink in front of Richard's nose. And he couldn't say no! When I saw him about midnight, he looked terrible. His face was white with panic. People were shouting, singing, and dancing all around him.

---

1. **had to** : was obliged to. Past of 'have to/must'.

Bizarre Tales

He couldn't escape. Then about fifteen minutes later he wasn't there.

'Where's Richard?' I asked Janet.

'Oh, he had to go,' she replied. 'He said he wasn't feeling well. What a pity! He was enjoying the party so much!'

A few nights later there was a knock at the door. When I opened it, I couldn't believe my eyes. It was Richard. He was standing in the wind and rain. He was as white as a sheet;[1] his eyes were dark and strange.

'Could you phone a doctor?' he said in a quiet voice. 'I'm not feeling well.'

I told him to come in and sit down. While I phoned, Janet made a cup of tea. Then she sat on the sofa with Richard. She was happy again.

'What's the matter?' she asked.

'I feel hot, I've got a headache, and my heart is beating fast.'

'Oh, you poor thing!' Janet said tenderly.

Dr Rockall arrived soon and examined Richard.

He said, 'You've got a fever[2] and your heartbeat is not regular. You must rest. Stay in bed for a few days. Relax and

---

1. **sheet** [ʃiːt] : large piece of cotton material. We put two of them on the bed to sleep in.
2. **fever** : temperature.

A Twentieth-Century Malady

eat plenty of ¹ good food. Here's some medicine for the fever.'

At the door he said to me, 'It may be a virus or perhaps an allergy. If he isn't better in a few days, call me.'

Of course Janet was really happy. She wanted Richard to sleep in our house but he said no. He wanted to go back to his house. So we took him next door ² and put him to bed. Now we could see inside the house for the first time – and we were amazed! He had tables, chairs, a sofa and armchair, carpets, bookcases, pictures, cupboards, etc. But there was no television set, no video recorder, no phone, no home computer, no hi-fi. There was nothing modern, not even electric lights. He had big candles in all the rooms.

He took the medicine and quickly fell asleep.

'I'm going to stay here and look after ³ him,' said Janet. 'Oh, look at this place! The poor boy hasn't got enough money to buy a telly. Let's get our old TV set. He can watch it in bed.'

'But Janet! He doesn't like TV.'

But she wasn't listening to me. I knew why she was doing these strange things. We haven't got any children and she wanted to give Richard all the kindness of a mother.

When he woke up and saw the TV at the end of the bed,

---

1. **plenty of** : a lot of.
2. **next door** : to the house next to ours.
3. **look after** : take care of.

Bizarre Tales

he looked frightened. He tried to move and speak but he was weak. [1]

'The doctor said you must rest,' smiled Janet. 'So be a good boy! Relax and watch TV. There's a quiz show, and then cartoons; then a comedy show, a soap opera, and an old film – a thriller I think.'

She made his pillow [2] comfortable and pulled the bedclothes tight. [3] He couldn't move. He stared at the TV with great frightened eyes, like a rabbit in front of a snake. [4]

'Are you hungry, Richard?' said Janet.

He tried to move his head but it was difficult.

'Good! You look so white and thin. You need some real food.'

Richard tried to shake his head. There was terror in his eyes.

'No, I won't listen to you, Richard! You're going to eat and eat and eat. Then you'll get big and strong.'

---

1. **weak** : opposite of strong.
2. **pillow** [pɪləʊ] : cushion used in bed.
3. **pulled the bedclothes tight** [taɪt] : put the sheets and blankets closely round him.
4. **rabbit in front of a snake** :

A Twentieth-Century Malady

Janet cooked some cream of chicken soup, and eggs and toast with lots of butter.

'Come on, don't be naughty,[1] Richard! Open your mouth. That's right! Eat up!' And Janet began to push the food into his mouth.

She stayed with Richard for six days and nights. She slept in the next room. She got a mobile phone for emergencies; but she called lots of friends and relatives and asked them to come and visit Richard. The phone was always ringing, people came and went, and it was very noisy. Then she got an old radio-cassette player from our house and Richard had to listen to music or radio programmes. She even decided to hire[2] a video recorder.

Richard was Janet's prisoner. He did everything she wanted. For six days he stayed in bed and watched TV and video films, or listened to loud music and the talk of visitors. His eyes were like glass, his face had no expression. He was like a zombie. Janet cooked him three big meals a day and he began to get fat. But he didn't get better. After ten days he was very weak. He didn't move and he didn't speak. He only stared in front of him.

1. **naughty** [nɔːti] : disobedient.
2. **hire** [haɪə] : pay money each day, week, etc. to be able to use.

Bizarre Tales

'Why doesn't he get better?' Janet asked Dr Rockall.

205 'It's strange. He looks better. He isn't thin and white now. Has he eaten well?'

'Oh yes! Lots and lots of good food.'

'Hm. The fever has gone down but his heart is still bad. I can't understand it. Look at his eyes. They look strange.
210 Perhaps he's asleep.'

'Oh, what shall we do, doctor?' Janet cried.

'Well, we can't take him to hospital. There aren't any free beds. We have to wait a few days. Perhaps I'll contact one of my colleagues [1] in Germany. Call me if there's any change.'

215 There was a change. Two days later a man arrived at our house. He was tall and strong, with a great black beard and a red face.

'My name is Doctor Hans von Rupprecht,' he said in a loud voice. He had a German accent. 'I am a good friend and
220 colleague of Dr Rockall. He phoned me yesterday about the mysterious malady of his patient Richard Jeffries. I had a patient in Germany with a similar malady. Is Mr Jeffries getting better?'

'No,' I said. 'He's becoming a vegetable.'

225 'A vegetable?'

'Yes. Vegetables aren't very lively, [2] are they?' I replied.

---

1. **colleagues** [kɒliːgz] : people who work in the same profession.
2. **lively** [laɪvli] : full of life or energy.

A Twentieth-Century Malady

'Do you know what's the matter with Richard?'

'Not precisely. But if my analysis is correct, it may be a new illness that has appeared only in the twentieth century. We don't know much about it but we have found that emissions from electronic objects like televisions, computers, videos, hi-fis, etc., probably cause it. It seems that the waves from these machines are not good for the brain and nerves. They change or disturb the electrical functions, but we don't know precisely how or why. There is fever and rapid heartbeats. The patient gradually passes into a coma.'

'Like a vegetable?'

'Yes! One strange symptom is that the patient wants to eat and drink a lot – usually fattening foods. You know, all the things that we eat today. So the patient becomes fat. We don't know why people need to eat a lot. Perhaps there are psychological causes. Nobody has done any experiments and nobody has written a scientific study. But we know the final result of the malady: the patient will die.'

At that moment there was a long, terrible scream from next door. Dr von Rupprecht and I ran out of the house. Janet was coming out of Richard's house. She was crying. When I asked her what was wrong, she couldn't answer. I

Bizarre Tales

put my arms round her and the doctor went into Richard's house. A few minutes later, he came out.

'He's dead,' he announced quietly. 'I found this under the pillow.'

It was an envelope. I opened it. There was a letter in it. I read it out to the others.

I'm going to die soon and I know that it's the twentieth century that is killing me.

Ten years ago, when I was eighteen, I was a very different person. I had a teenager's life-style. I went to discos with my friends every evening. I listened to loud music. I watched a lot of TV and videos. I liked computer games. I was always talking on the phone. Then something happened. I began to feel ill. I had bad headaches. My heartbeat was rapid. Sometimes I felt dizzy. I often had a temperature. I couldn't do my schoolwork. I didn't know why I was ill. I went to a doctor but he didn't know either. He said perhaps it was my life-style. I thought a lot about this. It was true that I never walked; I went everywhere by car. It was true that I drank a lot of alcohol and ate bad food. It was true that I watched a lot of stupid TV programmes – game shows, talk

A Twentieth-Century Malady

shows and hundreds of bad films. It was true that my ears weren't good because the music in the discos was very loud. It was true that I sat for hours in front of my computer. And it was true that I had started doing all these things when I was very young – about fourteen.

I took a lot of pills and medicine but I didn't get better. I became fat and very lazy. I never went out – except in the car. At weekends I sat in front of the TV all day or listened to music, and I ate and drank, drank and ate. I lived like a zombie. I never used my brain. It was full of the rubbish from TV programmes, silly songs and terrible films. I became very weak and very ill with a temperature and heart problems.

Then suddenly I understood. One day I had a little accident in the car and hit my head. It wasn't serious. But my mind became clear and I saw everything. I saw that the twentieth century was slowly killing me.

So I changed my life-style. I stopped living like a zombie. It was very difficult. My life-style was a habit – a very dangerous habit like taking drugs. Life at the end of the twentieth century was killing my mind and my body. So I

Bizarre Tales

began to walk everywhere. I didn't watch TV or listen to stupid music. I sold my computer and my video recorder. I didn't go to discos. I stopped eating bad food and drinking too much alcohol. And I lost all my friends too!

305 But the twentieth century was everywhere; it was too strong and I had to escape from it. So I came here to the country. But I couldn't escape. The twentieth century is too strong. I can't fight it. I know I'm going to die soon.

Goodbye.

310 *Richard Jeffries.*

When I finished, Dr von Rupprecht said sadly, 'So now we know that this is an illness of the mind caused by living in the twentieth century. Can I take this letter with me, please? I want to write a report about Richard's case and
315 publish it. Then all the world will know.'

But before the doctor could finish, poor Janet fell to the ground with a strange cry. Von Rupprecht examined her, then looked at me.

'She has got a temperature... her heartbeat is very fast!'
320 He shook his head sadly.

ACTIVITIES

After reading

1 Are these sentences true (T) or false (F)?

		T	F
a.	Reg and Janet wanted to help Richard because they were sorry for him.	✔	☐
b.	Richard didn't have a car because he was too poor.	☐	✔
c.	Reg and Janet ate a lot of rich food.	☐	☐
d.	Richard didn't want to come to dinner but he said yes.	☐	☐
e.	Janet liked vegetarian food.	☐	☐
f.	Richard had no job, no money, no friends or family, and no girlfriend.	☐	☐
g.	Janet understood Richard better than Reg did.	☐	☐
h.	Richard wasn't happy at the party because he didn't really want to go.	☐	☐
i.	When Dr Rockall examined Richard, he knew exactly what was wrong with him.	☐	☐
j.	Richard didn't have any modern things in his house because he was poor.	☐	☐
k.	Janet believed that she was helping Richard.	☐	☐
l.	Richard was very frightened but he couldn't escape from Janet.	☐	☐
m.	After ten days in bed Richard was fat and strong.	☐	☐
n.	Dr von Rupprecht already knew something about Richard's malady.	☐	☐
o.	Dr von Rupprecht said that scientists have done a lot of work on the illness.	☐	☐
p.	In his letter Richard said that normal life at the end of the twentieth century can be dangerous.	☐	☐
q.	The story seems to say that Janet's kindness to Richard was also dangerous.	☐	☐

ACTIVITIES

2 What differences are there between Richard at the beginning of the story and Richard ten years ago? Complete the column on the right. Remember – use the past tense!

At the beginning of the story Richard... But ten years ago...

a. always walks. He never walked.

b. hasn't got any friends. He had some friends.

c. is thin. ....

d. doesn't eat or drink very much. ....

e. never watches TV or video films. ....

f. hasn't got a computer. ....

g. doesn't drive a car. ....

h. never listens to loud music. ....

i. doesn't go to discos. ....

j. isn't studying at school. ....

3 A. Write who said:

WHO?

a. 'No, thank you. I prefer to walk.'

b. 'I think he (Richard) is happy.'

c. 'We only want to be kind to him.'

d. '*I'm* not going to invite him this time.'

e. 'Could you phone a doctor?'

f. 'Oh, what shall we do, doctor?'

g. 'I found this under the pillow.'

B. Now can you say why they said these things?

ACTIVITIES

4 A. Which adjectives are used for which person? Complete the table.

> kind   poor   ~~furious~~   frightened   German
> shy   thin   overweight   tall   disappointed
> quiet   strong   sad   offended   ill

Richard	Dr von Rupprecht	Janet	Reg
		furious	

B. Now complete the sentences with some of the adjectives in 4A.

a. Dr von Rupprecht spoke with a .... accent.

b. Reg and Janet eat a lot of good food so they are a bit ....

c. When Richard didn't eat the vegetarian dinner, Janet was a little ....

d. Reg and Janet wanted to be .... to Richard because they felt sorry for him.

e. Richard asked Reg to call a doctor because he felt ....

f. Janet said, 'Perhaps Richard is too .... to buy a car.'

g. Dr von Rupprecht was .... and ....

ACTIVITIES

5 A. Complete the table with the prepositions in the box.

> on   out   ~~into~~   down   to   ~~in~~   in front of
> under   out of   next to   ~~in~~

place	movement
in	into
	in

B. Now complete the sentences with all the prepositions in 5A.

a. Dr von Rupprecht went .... Richard's house and a few minutes later he came ....

b. Richard lived .... Reg and Janet.

c. 'Come .... and sit ...., Richard,' said Reg.

d. There was a letter .... the envelope.

e. Richard sat for hours .... the TV.

f. Richard is going .... the village to do some shopping.

g. Janet was coming .... Richard's house.

h. 'I found this .... the pillow,' said the doctor.

i. There is a lot of food .... Janet's plate.

ACTIVITIES

6 A. This food and drink is from the story. Can you label the pictures?

a. ....

b. ....

c. ....

d. ....

e. ....

f. ....

g. ....

h. ....

i. ....

j. ....

B. Now complete the sentences with much/many or a few/a little.

a. Richard doesn't eat .... eggs.
b. 'Would you like a .... wine, Richard?' said Janet.
c. How .... vegetables do you eat in a day?
d. 'Have we got any cakes, Janet?' 'Yes, there are a .... in the kitchen.'
e. 'Do you take sugar in your tea, Richard?' 'Yes, but not .... , thank you.'

ACTIVITIES

7 A. Listen to lines 143-51 and label the objects in the room. Write the names in the boxes, like the example.

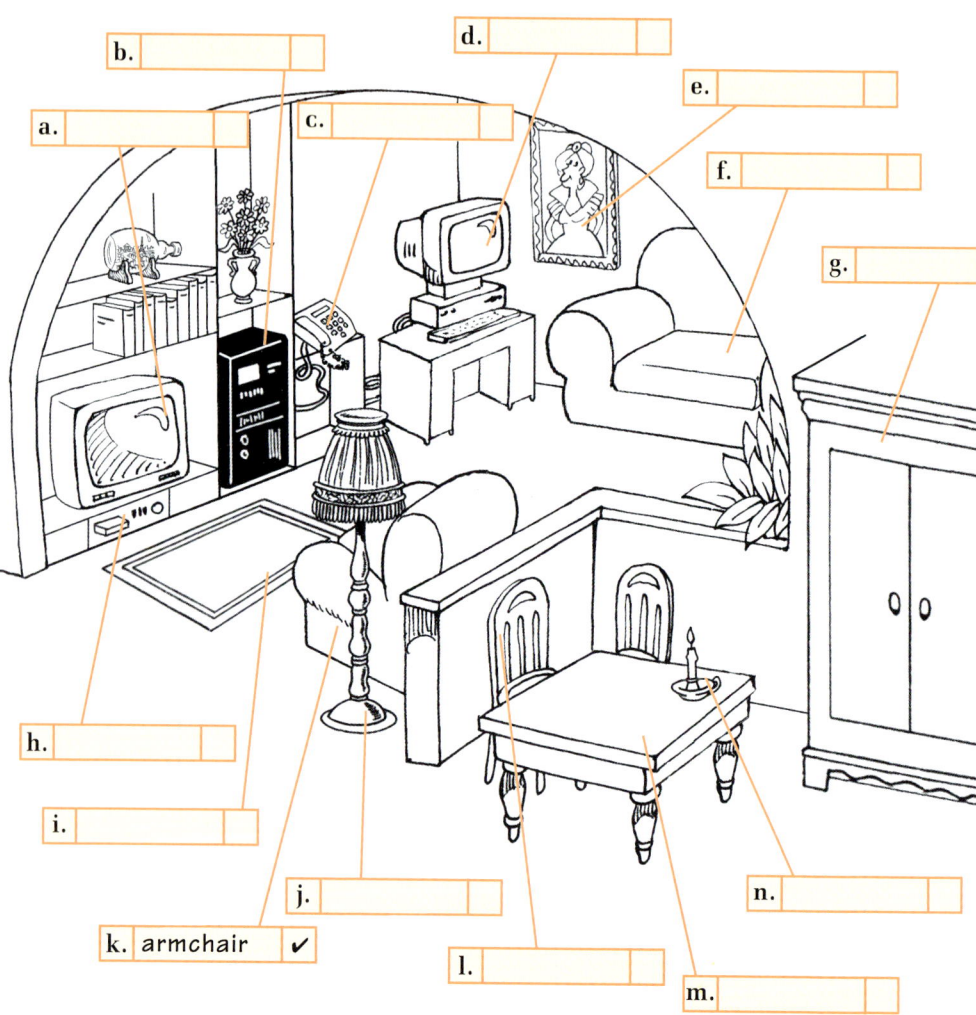

B. Now listen again and tick (✓) only the things that are in Richard's room, like the example.

ACTIVITIES

8 **Answer ONE of the following questions.**

   a. You are Dr Hans von Rupprecht. When you arrive in Germany, you write a report for a medical journal about Richard Jeffries's malady. Begin like this: 'I believe that a new illness has appeared in our century.'

   b. You are Reg. One day a cousin of Richard's arrives and asks to see him. Write a dialogue between you and the cousin. Explain what has happened – don't forget about Janet. Begin like this:

   Cousin: Hello, I'm Richard Jeffries's cousin. I live in Australia. I'm on holiday in Britain and I heard that he's living here. I would like to meet him...

9 **What is your opinion of the story? Tick (✓) any of the following. Give your reasons.**

- ☐ absurd
- ☐ interesting
- ☐ strange / bizarre
- ☐ boring
- ☐ incomprehensible
- ☐ incredible

Have you got the message?

Match the story to its message. Write a, b, c, etc. in the boxes.

a. Spirits of Place

b. God's Secret

c. The Boy Who Couldn't Sleep

d. Fiona's Spring Dress

e. A Twentieth-Century Malady

☐ Appearances are more acceptable to us than reality.

☐ The mass media are the opium of energy and intelligence.

☐ The original American civilization is still there under the surface.

☐ Behind accidental events there is a hidden purpose that we can't predict.

☐ The effects of electronic technology are dangerous to mind and body.

Notes

Notes

Notes

Notes

Notes

Notes